On the Track of a Mystery Horse!

In silence they scurried past the darkened main house. There was no moon, and once they were out of the reflection of the streetlight Jake could barely see Jody in front of him. They kept to the grass so that their sneakers would make no sound on the gravel driveway.

Once past the main house Jody and Jake ran in a half-crouch down the hill to the shed. Jake could feel his heart pounding in his chest. He was sure it was pounding loud enough to broadcast that they were there.

"We're going to have to go in through the window," said Jody, pointing to a small window that looked as if it dropped directly into the horse's stall.

"Oh, terrific!" said Jake. "Suppose he's keeping some killer horse in there and you just happen to drop in on him."

"Jake! Stop talking and give me a lift."

Jake cupped his hands to take Jody's foot and hoisted her so that she could grab the window's ledge with her hands. She could feel the warm, almost hot, breath of the horse right next to her. . . .

THE CASE OF THE COUNTERFEIT RACEHORSE

Elizabeth Levy

A JODY AND JAKE MYSTERY

#2

PUBLISHED BY POCKET BOOKS NEW YORK

Distributed in Canada by PaperJacks Ltd., a Licensee
of the trademarks of Simon & Schuster, a division of
Gulf ✛ Western Corporation.

Another *Original* publication of POCKET BOOKS

POCKET BOOKS, a Simon & Schuster division of
GULF & WESTERN CORPORATION
1230 Avenue of the Americas, New York, N.Y. 10020
In Canada distributed by PaperJacks Ltd.,
330 Steelcase Road, Markham, Ontario.

ISBN: 0-671-29965-4

First Pocket Books printing November, 1980

10 9 8 7 6 5 4 3 2 1

AN ARCHWAY PAPERBACK and ARCH are trademarks
of Simon & Schuster.

Printed in Canada

IL 5+

CONTENTS

THE CASE OF
THE COUNTERFEIT
RACEHORSE

1

"NO HORSE JOKES UNTIL NOON!"

Jody groaned. She stuck out her hand and hit the alarm button as hard as she could. It was only the second day of summer vacation, and here she was getting up before dawn. Jody and her brother Jake both had jobs at the racecourse this summer, and they had to be at the track at 6 A.M. Jody was *not* an early morning person. She pulled herself out of bed and groaned again.

The bathroom door was locked. "Jake!" whispered Jody hoarsely. "Get out of there."

"Hold your horses," said Jake in an impossibly cheery voice. A few seconds later Jake came out of the bathroom looking, from Jody's point of view, absurdly wide-awake. "That was a pun," he said. "Get it? . . . Hold your horses."

"I get it," mumbled Jody. "Just get out of the way."

Jake went downstairs and made bacon and eggs for breakfast. Jody came down and poured herself a huge glass of grapefruit juice. The sour-fresh taste helped. She looked out the window. It was still dark.

"I can't believe I'm awake at this hour," she said. "How did you talk me into this?"

"Me?" exclaimed Jake in a mock-innocent tone. "You're the one who loves animals. You leaped at the chance when I told you about the job."

"I can't leap before dawn," complained Jody.

"Come on," said Jake, "cheer up. Once you get to the track you can let the horses do the leaping." Jake threw back his head and began to sing: "Let your fingers do the walking, let your horses do the leaping."

"No songs! No jokes!" warned Jody. "I want to have a rule around here. No horse jokes until noon."

"Okay, okay. Just don't *nag* me about it," said Jake, ducking as Jody threw her napkin at him.

Harpo, the Markson's dog with the curly black hair of a poodle and the floppy ears of a spaniel, grabbed the napkin and shredded it. He looked up at Jody and wagged his tail wildly as if to say: "Let's play that napkin game again."

A horn sounded verly lightly outside. "That must be Peter and Mr. Barrett," said Jake, grabbing his windbreaker. A slightly battered green station wagon was waiting for Jody and Jake. In the driver's seat sat Mr. Barrett, a worried, tired-looking man with gray-blue eyes. Beside him sat his son Peter, a thin young man with powerful shoulders and biceps. He had a handsome, open face with wavy black hair, but he also had a strained look around his eyes, the same gray-blue color as his father's.

Jody and Jake tumbled into the back seat. Immmediately, both the younger and the older man put on a smile, but it was obviously put on. Whatever had been worrying or upsetting them was still there.

"Hi, Peter," said Jake. "How are you feeling, Mr. Barrett?"

"Fine, Jake," said Mr. Barrett, backing out of the driveway and seemingly deliberately avoiding Jake's eyes.

"How are you two feeling?" asked Peter. "Are you a little stiff from your first day on the job."

"Not too bad," said Jody. "If I survive getting up at this hour I'll be okay."

"You'll get used to it," said Peter, laughing, and he suddenly looked younger and more relaxed. Peter was one of Jake's best friends, even though he was sixteen, two years older than Jake. They had met at scout camp and almost instantly discovered they both had the same wacky sense of humor.

Peter was an apprentice jockey, and his father was a well-known trainer of racehorses. His mother had died when Peter was young. Mr. Barrett had suffered a heart attack in the spring. He had recovered, but he couldn't work as hard as he used to. Peter was trying to keep their string of horses together until his father had his full strength back. Peter needed all the help he could get, and Jody and Jake had signed on to work at the track for the summer.

As they drove out to the track, no one said anything. Both Peter and Mr. Barrett continued to seem very tense. Jody thought she could guess why. Racing was a very superstitious business, and owners of racehorses changed trainers very often. Even though Mr. Barrett was well enough to supervise the training and to make the major decisions, a lot of his owners were worried. Jody knew that he had lost much of his business since his heart attack.

At the gate to the track Buster Harris, the seventy-seven-year-old gateman, waved them through. Buster had done just about everything imaginable at the racetrack: trained horses, bred horses, rode as a jockey and gambled. Mostly gambled.

The sun was now peeping through the clouds. Jody looked around at all the horses being saddled up for their morning workouts. Buster grinned at them. "How are you feeling, Mr. Barrett," he asked.

"Much better," said Mr. Barrett. "How are you, Buster? Are you thinking of retiring?"

"No. They're going to have to carry me out feet first," said Buster with a smile. "This is the life for me!"

Mr. Barrett seemed cheered up by Buster's words. His shoulders and neck relaxed as he drove along into the backstretch, the area of the track where the horses were stabled. He half turned to Jody and Jake in the back seat. "I always love it here at this hour," he said. He pointed to a group of horses doing a gallop. "Look at them. Some look half awake, some look lazy, some look sore, but you can always tell the runners. They always look ready."

Jody looked out at the horses. To her unschooled eyes, the horses didn't look that different. She could tell the difference in color, all right: the bays from the chestnuts, the occasional gray —although gray was considered an unlucky color at the racetrack. But she didn't have Mr. Barrett's practiced eye. To her, all thoroughbreds looked like runners, with their thin, delicate ankles and powerful hindquarters, built for speed.

Mr. Barrett parked his station wagon in a place reserved for trainers. Each trainer was assigned a different barn at the track, and trainers like Mr. Barrett, who often had several horses running each afternoon, would be given the best barn.

As he walked to the barn Jody noticed his shoulders sagged just a little. "Is your father all right?" Jody whispered to Peter.

"Another owner took his horse away from us last night," said Peter sadly.

Jody couldn't think of anything to say to cheer up Peter. She knew that if Mr. Barrett's business didn't pick up, he wouldn't make it through the summer, and she and Jake would be out of a job.

2
A STRANGE
NEW HORSE

Jody was an excellent horseback rider. Riding had been her favorite activity at summer camp, and she had often won blue ribbons in camp shows. But racing and horse shows were two completely different worlds. Racing, Jody realized, was like an island that existed completely off on its own, with a separate set of rules, a separate and elaborate language, and most of all, a separate money system.

Money.

The amounts staggered Jody and Jake. Even the slowest horse Mr. Barrett trained cost thousands of dollars. Millions of dollars exchanged hands every day at the track. It was like entering an Alice-in-Wonderland world where real money was treated as if it were colored monopoly paper.

Walking through the backstretch, Jody was

struck by the contrast between all that money and the sight in front of her. The barns in the backstretch were full of cobwebs and barn swallows. Almost everyone was dressed in blue jeans and old clothes. Boots were the most expensive item anyone wore, but they were hidden by layers of dirt and muck.

"Are you still asleep?" whispered Jake. "You look like you're in a daze."

"No, I'm awake," said Jody. "I was just thinking about all the money in racing. It's crazy."

"I know what you mean," commented Peter. He pushed his hair back from his eyes. "I remember the first time I rode a $50,000 horse. I felt like I was riding Fort Knox."

"Did you win?" asked Jake.

"Nope," said Peter good-naturedly. "I lost to a cheaper nag. Come on, you know I haven't won a race yet."

"But you will . . . this summer!" Jake twisted his head around as if looking around for eavesdroppers. "Hey, Jody," he whispered in perfect imitation of some of the gamblers who hung around the track in the early morning, "do you want a hot tip? Peter Barrett is going to win his first race. Soon!"

Peter laughed, but there was a bitter edge in his voice. "My dad used to get the best horses to train. We had a couple of winners every season. But now, most of the owners are sending their horses to other trainers. They think my father just doesn't have 'it' anymore, that he's too sick. None of the horses we're training now really have a chance of winning. They could have a hurricane blowing behind them, and they'd still come in last."

"If they had Hurricane Jody behind them, they'd run faster," said Jake.

"Now that they're naming hurricanes after guys, I'm waiting for Hurricane Jake," said Jody.

"Speaking of hurricanes," said Peter, "we'd better hurry, or my father will *cane* us. We've got a lot of work to do this morning."

Jody groaned. "No wonder you and Jake are friends," she moaned. "I may not survive a summer of puns."

At the Barrett's barn, Mr. Barrett was waiting for them in the tack room, a curiously homey looking room for a barn. The saddles and bridles were neatly lined up on the wall, looking almost like an interior decorator had placed them on display. A worn-looking but clean, comfy sofa lined the wall, and there was a TV set in the corner. Mr. Barrett stood in front of his desk, moodily staring at a chart on his wall. The chart listed the names of all the horses in Mr. Barrett's care and a symbol for what each horse was supposed to do that day—work, gallop, walk or rest. But heavy black lines crisscrossed the chart, indicating horses that had been taken away.

Some trainers were known for pushing their horses too hard. They hoped to win one big race, and sometimes they did. But their horses often broke down soon afterward with sore legs or ruined wind. Mr. Barrett believed in a much slower process. He was a trainer who loved horses, and horses loved him. He carefully planned each horse's schedule, never pushing a horse beyond its endurance. His horses won more races in the long run, but owners were often impatient to see a big win before the horse was ready.

"What do you want me to do today, Dad?" asked Peter.

"I want 'Gotta Wanna' to walk," said Mr. Barrett. "Jake can ride him." Jake was the least experienced rider of the three. To tell the truth, Jake did not exactly love horses, but he was excited by the track and the gambling. Jake was an excellent poker player. He had been ever since his mom had taught him when he was seven. They always played for pretzels because Jake liked them more than peanuts. Mrs. Markson wouldn't let him play for money. Jody played poker too, but Jake was the one who loved to figure out the mathematical odds of different poker hands. Jake found racing just as fascinating. It was against the law for minors to bet at the track, but Jake enjoyed making bets in his head.

"Okay," said Jake, "I wanna get on Gotta Wanna!"

"Jake," said Mr. Barrett with a smile, "it's bad enough the owners gave that poor horse a silly name."

"I'll help you saddle him up," said Peter.

"Good," said Mr. Barrett. "Then I want Jody to take Gallant Dancer out for a slow gallop."

"Now that's a name for a horse!" said Jody.

"I agree," said Mr. Barrett.

"Peter, you take So Talented out for a full gallop. I'll see to a few things around the barn and then I'll saddle up a horse and come watch you."

"Are you sure you should, Dad?" asked Peter worriedly. "The doctors didn't say you could ride."

"The doctors don't have to meet my bills," said Mr. Barrett, "or for that matter pay their own bills." Mr. Barrett glanced up from his desk. He saw how much he had upset Peter. "Now, come on, son," he said, "don't put on such a long face. We're going to be all right."

"I'm not worried about the money," said Peter. "I'm worried about your getting sick again."

Mr. Barrett smiled, but he looked uncomfortable, as if he didn't like talking about his problems in front of Jody and Jake.

Jody sensed how he felt. "I'll go saddle up Gallant Dancer," she said. She turned to leave the tack room. To her surprise a strange horse was standing in the passageway, blocking the light. The horse looked huge. A tall man was holding the lead line slackly.

"Excuse me," said Jody, and she carefully moved around the horse. Suddenly she screamed. She felt as if a metal vice had grabbed her arm.

11

The horse had his teeth on her forearm; he just grabbed hold and wouldn't open up.

Jake, Peter and Mr. Barrett rushed out of the tack room. The man holding the horse tried to make the horse let go, but the horse held on to Jody's arm, as if he had just found something that belonged to him.

"Help!" cried Jody. "He won't let go."

3

A MISTREATED HORSE

The horse began to shake its head. Jody felt sweat trickle down her back.

"Here you! Let go!" commanded Mr. Barrett. He smacked the horse hard between the eyes. The horse opened its mouth, and Jody pulled her arm away.

"Are you all right?" asked the man who had been holding the horse.

Jody felt her arm. The horse's teeth hadn't broken her skin, but there were five red marks where the horse's teeth had sunk in, and her arm hurt. She had to fight hard not to cry.

Mr. Barrett turned to the man holding the horse. "Doc, what is that horse doing here?"

"Hold on, Jared," said the man. "I brought this horse over to you for its new owner. I told the owner you were the best person to train him. I didn't know it would bite the arm off your new stable gal."

"Jody, meet Doc Connelly," said Mr. Barrett. He's one of the best vets around, but he should have known better than to just bring a strange horse into my barn with no warning."

"Now, Jared, don't get so excited," said Dr. Connelly. "Your gal, Jody, looks like a strong lass." Dr. Connelly was a familiar figure around the racetrack. He was a big man, but not fat. He smiled often and laughed even more. He was known to be a gossip, but racing people love gossip, so that was never held against him.

Dr. Connelly handed the reins to Mr. Barrett while he examined Jody's arm. "At least he didn't break the skin. Peter, go get some ice to put on her arm."

"I'm okay," said Jody in a shaky voice. "I think I was shocked more than anything else."

Meanwhile, Mr. Barrett was staring at the horse. "I'm not sure I want a horse around here who likes to take bites out of people's arms," he complained.

"I didn't think you were in a position to turn down new owners," said Dr. Connelly.

Peter came back with ice in a towel and handed it to Jody. "Dad's bluffing," he whispered. "He doesn't want Doc Connelly to know how desperate we are."

"You can't blame him for being proud," whispered Jody.

Mr. Barrett sighed. "Let's take this horse out in the sunshine where I can get a good look at him."

Outside, the horse turned out to be a poor specimen of horseflesh. His chestnut coat looked dull and unhealthy. He was a good size, over sixteen hands, but his legs looked raw and infected, with grapefruit-size knees. He tossed his head around nervously.

"Easy, easy," murmured Mr. Barrett as he ran his hand expertly down the horse's leg. The horse tried to bite Mr. Barrett, but he stepped out of the way.

"He's a mean-tempered animal," Mr. Barrett muttered. "Somebody's been treating him awfully badly."

"He's been imported from England," said Dr. Connelly. "I don't know the name of his trainer over there. His owner is willing to pay you double your daily rate."

Mr. Barrett looked up sharply. "Why should he pay me double?" he asked.

"*She.* She's a wealthy doctor. You know owners—they get crazy ideas. I told her that you were the best person around to take on a horse that had been mistreated and make him sound. She checked your reputation around the track, and everyone agreed with me. She doesn't want anyone else to train this horse."

Mr. Barrett looked at Doc Connelly suspiciously. "Are you sure this isn't your idea? You know I don't want charity."

"Jared, stop being so touchy," said Dr. Connelly. "You're turning into a prickly cactus plant. I told the owner the honest truth. If anyone can turn this horse around, you can."

"He's right, Dad," Peter chimed in. "You are the best man for the job."

Mr. Barrett just shook his head as he looked over the horse with his practiced eye. "I can't see this nag winning too many races."

"He's got some good blood in him," said Dr. Connelly. "His mother was one of the top steeplechasers in England a few years back, and they bred her to a horse with good speed. He should be strong and fast."

"He looks weak and slow," mumbled Jake. Jody nodded. There was something so sad about the way the horse stood, shaking his head nervously, trying to move away from the sun.

"I think he doesn't like the sun in his eyes," Jody suggested.

"Maybe . . . but most horses love the sunlight . . . just like people," said Mr. Barrett. "I'm not sure what's bothering him."

"What's his name?" Jody asked.

"Pure Energy," said Dr. Connelly.

"Poor Energy would describe him better," whispered Jake.

"I wouldn't joke if I were you," said Peter. "You might be assigned to clean out his stall."

"Not me," said Jake. "I don't want to get my arm bitten off."

"Here comes the owner now, Dr. Mary Grant."

To Jody's surprise the owner seemed quite young, in her late twenties. She wore designer jeans and a beautifully fitted plaid western shirt. She wore her hair long and loose. She had an arrogant air about her, as if she thought she belonged in a TV commercial.

"We had trouble finding you," complained Dr. Grant. "Your stable's sort of tucked away."

"I know, but it's the only one at the track that has a southern exposure," said Mr. Barrett calmly. "Horses like sunlight, and I always try to get one that faces south."

"That's very nice," said Dr. Grant impatiently, "but can you make a winner out of Pure Energy. That's what counts."

"He's in pretty bad shape," said Mr. Barrett. "We'll have to fatten him up and get him calmed down before we can see what kind of speed he's capable of. What's his record so far?"

"He hasn't won a race yet, ever—not even in England," said Dr. Connelly.

"Neither has Peter," said Mr. Barrett. "Maybe we can put the two of them together."

"Hey," said Jake, "maybe it'll be the right combination. I would bet on Peter and Pure Energy. They sound like they go together."

"More money than you can count has been lost on just such stupid bets like that," said Mr. Barrett. But he smiled. Jody knew that he was glad to have a customer again.

"He could be a dark horse," said Jake. "In fact, he is sort of a dark horse."

"He's a dark horse in color," said Mr. Barrett. "But as for being *the* dark horse, I wouldn't bet on it. In fact, I'm glad minors aren't allowed to bet. I'd hate to see you lose your money."

"Where does the phrase 'dark horse' come from?" Jody asked.

Mr. Barrett looked at Pure Energy. "Well, come to think of it, it does come from English racing. It means the horse that nobody expects to win."

"Well, that fits Pure Energy," admitted Jody.

4

THE LOOK OF
AN EAGLE

"Your arm looks better," said Mrs. Markson. "Finally. For a while I thought it was turning into a purple cabbage."

"It never hurt as bad as it looked," said Jody, rubbing her arm where Pure Energy had bitten her. The purple bruises on Jody's arm had faded in the two and a half weeks since Pure Energy had joined the stable.

"He has his first race tomorrow," said Jake. "Peter is going to ride him. Can you come?"

"What time will it be?" asked Mrs. Markson. "I have to be in court in the morning, but if I can get away I'd like to come. I haven't been to the races in years." Mrs. Markson was a criminal lawyer, and Jody and Jake often became involved in her cases.

"He won't be running until the fifth race," said Jody. "I get to take him around the paddock."

"Jody's practically the only one who can go near him. He likes her."

"Likes her!" exclaimed Mrs. Markson. "That bruise on her arm doesn't make me think he likes her. I'm worried about your being around such a mean horse."

"I don't think he's really mean. I think his trainer in England mistreated him," said Jody.

They were sitting around the dining room table. Mrs. Markson was slicing up the chocolate cake she had bought. Normally, Jake did most of the cooking in the house. Mrs. Markson was divorced. Jody and Jake's father was a psychologist living in New York, and Jody and Jake visited him in the summer sometimes. Jake was a very good cook, but the combination of getting up at 5:30 and the hard physical labor at the track made him too tired to cook at night. Mrs. Markson had decided that she would cook all their meals. However, because she did not like to cook, this meant they ate a lot of TV dinners.

Mrs. Markson looked at her two children critically. "You both look awfully tired. Are you sure this job isn't too much for you?"

"No, Mom . . . we love it," said Jody. "I'm even getting used to getting up in the morning. It's just . . ." Jody's voice trailed off.

"Something is bothering you," said Mrs. Markson. "I can tell. Is Mr. Barrett all right?"

"He seems to feel okay," said Jake. "But he's depressed. You can't blame him. The owners are convinced that he's not as good as he was before he got sick."

"What about the owner of Pure Energy?" asked Mrs. Markson. "He seems to have faith in him."

"She," corrected Jody. "Pure Energy belongs to a woman doctor. I don't think she ever owned a racehorse before. She doesn't seem to like Pure Energy very much. She's insisting he race tomorrow. Mr. Barrett would have liked to rest him some more."

"Well, I guess all owners are impatient," said Mrs. Markson. "They've paid tremendous money for a horse. They want to see if it will pay off."

"Jody just wants Pure Energy to lead a life of luxury," said Jake.

"I do not!" protested Jody. "I just would like him to have a chance to recover, that's all."

"Well, just make sure he doesn't take another bite of your arm tomorrow," warned Mrs. Markson. "I'll try to get to the track as soon as I can."

The next morning Mr. Barrett and Peter picked up Jody and Jake even earlier than usual. Harpo came bounding out to the car.

"I want to get to the track early," said Mr. Barrett. "I want to make sure that Pure Energy stays relaxed this morning."

"How are you going to see to that?" asked

Peter. "That horse hasn't relaxed once since we've gotten him."

"I know," said Mr. Barrett. "He's a nervous eater. They're the worst kind. I just hope this race doesn't do him any harm."

When Jody opened the car door to get in, Harpo jumped inside. "Go back, Harpo. Go inside," commanded Jody.

"Oh, you can bring him along," said Mr. Barrett. "Maybe he'll bring us good luck."

"Are you sure?" asked Jody.

"Of course," said Mr. Barrett. "We always used to have a dog around our stables, but somehow I got out of the habit. Maybe Harpo will change my luck."

"I bet he will," said Jody.

"Want to bet on it," said Peter cynically.

"What's the matter, Peter? Don't you think you're going to win today?" asked Jake.

Peter laughed. "I'll be lucky if that horse doesn't throw me. When I've taken him out for workouts, it was all I could do to keep him in control."

"I just hope this race doesn't do him any harm," repeated Mr. Barrett, driving into the track.

When they got to the shed rows, the few other horses in Mr. Barrett's care were all facing out, waiting for their early meal. Only Pure Energy stood aloof, facing away from the light, staring at the rear wall.

As Mr. Barrett opened his stall to look at him, Pure Energy pinned his ears back. He rolled back his lips. His teeth, stained and brown, were not a pretty sight. "Easy, big boy, easy," murmured Mr. Barrett in a soothing voice. Suddenly, Harpo bounded into the stall, wagging his tail.

"Hey, Harpo, get out of there!" whispered Jody urgently. "You'll get kicked."

Harpo went right up to Pure Energy, jumped up and licked Pure Energy on the nose.

"You're going to get yourself killed," warned Jody, grabbing Harpo's collar and pulling him away.

"Wait a minute, Jody," said Mr. Barrett in a soft voice. "Look at Pure Energy."

Pure Energy's ears perked up, and he had turned to face Harpo. He was standing very calmly. He brought down his great neck and extended his muzzle toward Harpo as if he wanted to play.

Harpo was straining at his collar to try to get back to Pure Energy.

"What's going on?" asked Jake, peering into the stall.

"I think we've got a case of love at first sight," said Mr. Barrett smiling. "I've seen stranger things at the racecourse. Horses often take to a particular dog or a cat. I just never thought of Pure Energy as that kind of a horse."

Jody let go of Harpo's collar. Pure Energy

flicked his ears again and playfully nuzzled Harpo. Harpo's tail never stopped wagging.

"Well," said Mr. Barrett, "I want him to have just a light meal this morning. Give him a scoop of rolled oats and half a scoop of sweet feed. Then we'll take him out for a short walk and get him groomed up for his big day."

"Okay, Mr. Barrett," said Jody. "Should I just leave Harpo in his stall?"

"Why not?" said Mr. Barrett. "It looks like those two get along. Maybe Harpo will be just the calming influence I've been looking for."

Jody fed Pure Energy and then went on with her other chores. When the time came to get Pure Energy ready for his race, Jody brought him outside. His legs still looked swollen. Mr. Barrett came out and carefully wrapped up all four of Pure Energy's legs in flannel bandages that had been soaked in ice water. "That will help keep the swelling down," he said.

Just as he had finished wrapping the last legs, Dr. Grant came over to see her horse. "Why are you bandaging his forelegs?" demanded Dr. Grant. She was wearing thigh-high blue cowboy boots with hand-embroidered flowers on them— cowboy boots that no cowboy would even want to be seen dead in.

"I said, why are you bandaging his legs?" Dr. Grant repeated, hardly giving Mr. Barrett a chance to answer.

Mr. Barrett looked up slowly. "Because his legs

are still swollen, and I want him to come out of this race as sound as possible."

"But he looks like an accident case like that," protested Dr. Grant. "If you send him out like that, nobody will bet on him. Everyone will think he's a loser."

"Dr. Grant, why do you want other people to bet on him?" asked Jody. "I know that some people don't like to bet on horses who have bandages on their front legs, but why should that matter to you? If you think Pure Energy will win, the fewer people that bet on him, the higher odds you get. Isn't that right, Jake?"

"Yeah. I talked Mom into placing a bet on Pure Energy for us. So that's at least one bet he's got. But I'm hoping nobody else does."

Dr. Grant looked flustered. "Well, I just don't like the way those bandages look."

"They stay," said Mr. Barrett firmly. Then he seemed to remember that Dr. Grant was paying his bills, and he became a little more polite.

"Actually, I'm quite pleased with Pure Energy today. He seems to have found himself a mascot. Harpo, here, is Jody's dog, and Pure Energy seems to have taken a fancy to him. It shows he's beginning to come out of his shell."

As if he understood that he was being talked about, Pure Energy shook his head. His eyes looked bright and clear. For the first time Jody could see a hint of the "look of an eagle" that Mr. Barrett said all thoroughbreds should have.

5

A TRIPLE BUG

Jody washed and brushed Pure Energy's coat until it gleamed. She laced green ribbons into his mane to set off the reddish tints in his coat. As she worked, Pure Energy moved about restlessly.

"Shhh," whispered Jody. "You have to save your energy for the race. Do you think you're going to win?"

Pure Energy shook his head from side to side so vigorously that the sponge fell from Jody's hand. Jake laughed. "I would not say that Pure Energy has much confidence. That was a clear case of a horse saying no."

"Pure Energy always shakes his head like that," protested Jody. "It doesn't mean a thing."

Just then, Peter and Mr. Barrett came out of the tack room. Peter was dressed in Pure Energy's racing colors: green and gold. "You look terrific," said Jody, "but I've got to warn you; Pure Energy just shook his head no when I asked him if he was going to win."

Peter laughed. "That's going straight to the horse's mouth."

"Well, I still think he has a chance," insisted Jody.

Mr. Barrett put his arm around Jody's shoulder. "You've got him looking beautiful, Jody. And you've got the right spirit. Only, the one thing you must learn around the track is that every horse can't be a winner."

"But Peter will try, won't he?" Jody asked anxiously.

"Hey, Jody, what do you take me for?" asked Peter, sounding a bit angry. "Of course I'm going to try. I want him to win as much as you do. Probably more."

"I'm sorry," said Jody quickly. "I didn't mean that I thought you were trying to lose."

"Come on, now," said Mr. Barrett, "enough of this talk about losing. It's time to get you and Pure Energy to the paddock. Are you ready for your first public display?"

Before each race, the horses are displayed to the public in a ring behind the grandstand called the paddock. Jody had purposely taken a clean pair of jeans and a new shirt to wear as she paraded Pure Energy in front of would-be bettors.

Mrs. Markson waved from the paddock fence. Another woman was standing by the fence talking to her. Jody nodded, but she didn't dare take her attention away from Pure Energy. His tail was swishing nervously from side to side. The crowds seemed to worry him and his eyes darted back and forth. Every once in a while, Pure Energy would dig his hooves into the ground, acting like a child being dragged into the doctor's office for a polio shot.

There were only six other horses in the race. Jake went up to his mother. "Ssst! Want a hot tip? Bet on the horse with the green ribbons. Those green ribbons have a concealed electric shock in them, and that horse is going to go like lightning."

The woman standing next to Mrs. Markson overheard Jake and carefully wrote something down in her notebook.

"Wait a minute," said Mrs. Markson, smiling. "That was just my son's idea of a joke."

The woman laughed. "Don't worry," she said. "I've heard of strange electric gadgets around the track, but even I don't believe in magical green ribbons."

The woman looked down at her program and then back up at the number on Pure Energy's saddlecloth. "Pure Energy? I see he's being ridden by a triple bug."

"I beg your pardon," said Mrs. Markson, slightly offended. "That exaggerated bug you're talking about happens to be my son's best friend."

The woman laughed. She was a tall woman

with glasses, in her early thirties, and she somehow didn't look as if she belonged at the racetrack. Most of the women regulars were older and
had a somewhat sadder look to their faces.

"I wasn't insulting your friend," the woman
said to Jake. "I just noticed that the jockey on
Pure Energy is still an apprentice. That means
Pure Energy won't have to carry as much weight.
They give horse ridden by apprentices a weight
advantage."

"Yeah, that's right," said Jake, "Peter told me.
But why did you call it a bug?"

The woman pointed to her program.

FIFTH RACE

Dr. M. GRANT	JARED BARRETT	50-1
Emerald green and gold diamonds, green sleeves, green cap		PETER BARRETT

5 PURE ENERGY   ***117

CH. c3, Raise the Flag; Keep the Peace by Merry Union

"Do you see those three asterisks by 117? Well,
that means your friend weighs 117 pounds and
he is going to be allowed to use a very light saddle
and have no extra weight. His horse will be carrying 10 pounds less than the other horses. Beginning jockeys are allowed 10 pounds until they
win five races. The horse that he is riding has
never won a race either."

Mrs. Markson held up her program so she

could study it. "It looks as complicated as a law book," she said.

"I know," said the woman. "I should introduce myself. I'm Liz Gerber. I help make out the programs. We do try to cram a lot of information into a little space. It's like a code. But you can find out almost everything you need to know. For example, it tells you that Pure Energy is owned by Dr. Grant, and trained by Jared Barrett. Peter Barrett is the jockey and he's going to be wearing an emerald green shirt with gold diamonds and green sleeves and a green cap. When you are watching a race it's much easier to look for the jockey's colors than it is to read the number on a jockey's back. That's why races are so colorful."

"What does 'CH, c3' mean?" asked Jake. "And 'Raise the Flag'?"

"CH stands for Chestnut. So Pure Energy's a chestnut horse and he's a colt, not a filly, and three years old. Raise the Flag was his father, Keep the Peace was his mother and Merry Union is his grandfather on his mother's side."

"It *is* as complicated as law," exclaimed Mrs. Markson.

Liz Gerber laughed. "I know, and the arguments can get just as petty, but we try to give people all the information they need to make an intelligent bet."

"At odds of 50-to-1 it may not be an intelligent bet, but I think I'll put a sentimental two dollars on Pure Energy," said Mrs. Markson.

Liz Gerber frowned. "I'm afraid you'll be throwing your money away. His blood lines are weak, and there are other horses in the race who look much better."

"Well, I haven't made a bet in ten years," said Mrs. Markson, "and my daughter Jody seems to have a real feeling for Pure Energy."

"Not to mention her feelings for Peter," added Jake.

"Hey, no teasing your sister," said Mrs. Markson. "If she likes Peter, it's none of your business."

"Excuse me," said Liz Gerber, "but if you want to place your bet, you'd better do it now."

Mrs. Markson headed for the window to place her two dollar bet. She came back just as the trumpet sounded for the start of the race.

Even from the stands it was obvious that Peter was having a hard time controlling Pure Energy as they walked to the starting gate. "Walked" was not the right word for what Pure Energy was doing. He was using up precious energy by nervously hopping from one foot to the other. Mr. Barrett had one of the grooms ride on a pony beside Pure Energy, but the calmer, older horse did nothing for Pure Energy's nerves. By the time he reached the starting gate he had worked up a lather.

Luckily, he seemed to calm down in the starting gate, and Peter had little trouble getting him into the right slot. He broke well too, coming out of the starting gate just a second after the buzzer.

But almost immediately, Pure Energy was in trouble. Peter allowed himself to get crowded between two horses and he had to drop back into the pack. After that, Pure Energy never seemed to have a chance.

By the time he got to the stretch Pure Energy had almost no energy at all left. Jody, who was watching with Mr. Barrett at the rails, could clearly see how tired Pure Energy was. His tail drooped, and his gait was awkward and out of rhythm. He looked like a tired boxer coming out for the tenth round.

Mr. Barrett just shook his head sadly.

Mrs. Markson tore up a ticket she held in her hand.

"What's that?" asked Jody.

"Two dollars down the drain," said Mrs. Markson.

"It's a pity," said Mr. Barrett. "I wish you had asked me. I would have told you not to bet on him, even though I trained him. More money has been lost foolishly at the track than down dry oil wells. I've got something of a reputation as an old puritan about this, but I hate to see people lose their money at the track. I've seen too many lives ruined."

6

AN EXPENSIVE BUNCH OF NERVES

Dr. Grant looked furious as she paced up and down in front of the stables, waiting for Peter to bring Pure Energy to the backstretch. Dr. Connelly was with her, trying to calm her down.

"Now, now, it was his first race in this country. You can't expect too much."

"I could have beat him without a horse," said Dr. Grant, "running on my own two feet!"

"I would like to see her try," muttered Jake, "especially in those boots."

Jody ignored him. "I'm sure Peter did his best," she said to Dr. Grant, "and remember, Mr. Barrett said he wasn't ready."

Dr. Grant turned on Jody furiously. "I paid a lot of money for Pure Energy and, despite what some people might think, I did not buy him for a tax loss. I expect him to win his keep."

"And he will," said Dr. Connelly soothingly. "You have the very best trainer for that horse that I could imagine. If anyone can get Pure Energy into shape, Jared can. You've got to give him time. Jared has never been the kind of a trainer to push his horses toward one race and burn them out. He tries to get a good performance each and every race. You just have to trust him."

"That may have been true in the past," snapped Dr. Grant, "but I've heard rumors that since his heart attack he's not the same man."

"That's not true!" exclaimed Jody, so angry that she had to say somthing. Dr. Grant just ignored her and continued pacing up and down between the sheds.

"Shhh," warned Jake, "I don't think she likes being contradicted."

"I think she's awful," said Jody.

"Yeah," said Jake, "but she pays the bills, so she's the boss."

Peter and Mr. Barrett brought Pure Energy back to the barn. He was covered with sweat and he was limping slightly.

"Is he all right?" Jody asked.

"He's okay. You'd better get him walking to cool down," said Mr. Barrett.

Pure Energy followed Jody willingly. He seemed too tired to put up any of his usual protest.

"You did your best, Pure Energy," she whispered. "The next race you'll do better."

Pure Energy shook his head up and down as if agreeing with her.

"See, Mr. Barrett, Pure Energy just said he was going to win the next time."

Mr. Barrett laughed. "Well, he'll have to do better than today."

"He just ran out of energy at the end, Dad," said Peter. "It was as if had nothing left."

"You let yourself get boxed in at the beginning," complained Dr. Grant.

"I did," admitted Peter, "but that lasted for only a second. We had the room to move for most of the race, but Pure Energy didn't have anything left to give."

Mr. Barrett sighed. Keeping up good relations with difficult owners was by far the hardest part of his job. But he couldn't allow Dr. Grant to become too angry.

"I'm sure if you just give me a chance to rest Pure Energy, he'll come around," said Mr. Barrett.

Jody continued to walk Pure Energy around in circles. Jake kept her company.

"He's already coming around," Jake whispered.

"Do you think he knows that he lost?" asked Jody.

"He just looks like a sweating horse to me," said Jake.

Peter had moved away from his father and Dr. Grant and joined them. "If she had her way, she'd run that horse into the ground," muttered Peter. He rested his hand on Pure Energy's flank.

Pure Energy shook his head restlessly. Harpo trotted by his side, wagging his tail.

Suddenly, Jody was aware of Dr. Connelly's voice speaking rather forcefully. "I tell you what, Jared. Why don't I take him over to my place and give him a thorough checkup?"

"I think that's a good idea," said Dr. Grant. "Perhaps there's something physically wrong with him."

"Why don't you check him here, Doc?" said Mr. Barrett. "I don't think it's good for the horse to keep moving him from place to place. I'd like to give him a feeling of security. He's had a lot of changes in his life lately. He's been shipped from England. He's had to get used to a new climate, new people. He's just begun to settle down. That Jody Markson has been good for him. She and that horse just click."

"Wasn't she the one whom he bit that first day?"

"Yes," said Mr. Barrett. "She's still got the black-and-blue marks on her arm from it. But she's got a gentle manner around that horse. And he's the better for it. I'd like to keep Pure Energy here in the stall that he knows. You can do any tests you want here."

Dr. Grant looked annoyed. "That sounds like sentimental nonsense about a girl and her horse. Actually, it's my horse. If that horse is attached to anybody, it's me. I paid for him."

Mr. Barrett bit his tongue to keep from saying that money had never bought a horse's loyalty. "Nonetheless," said Mr. Barrett firmly, "I don't like Pure Energy to be taken from our barn."

Dr. Grant turned away from him furiously. She turned to Dr. Connelly as if expecting support. "Now, Jared," said Doc Connelly soothingly. "I think you're being a little too serious about this whole issue. I'll tell you what. Why don't I bring my horse trailer around and you can have the girl load him herself? That should calm him down."

"I'll be glad to go with him," volunteered Jody. "I can ride in the back of the trailer and Harpo can go too. That way Pure Energy will feel almost as if he were at home."

For a second, Jody thought she saw a look of anger flash across Dr. Connelly's normally good-natured face. Then she looked again and it was gone, and she was convinced she had been mistaken. "I don't think it's necessary for Jody to go all the way to my office with me. It's a two-hour drive from the track."

"That's all the more reason for me to go," protested Jody. "Pure Energy could get very upset during two hours locked up in a horse trailer."

"I agree," said Mr. Barrett. "If you don't mind, I'd like to have her go along."

"But how will she get back," said Dr. Connelly impatiently. "I won't be able to drive her back home."

"I'll go get her," said Peter. "I just got my license and I could use the practice."

"Doesn't your father need you around here, Peter?" asked Dr. Connelly.

"No, I can manage," said Mr. Barrett testily, not liking the implication that he was too sick to take care of his stable on his own.

"I don't understand why there is all this fuss about just taking a horse to the vet's for some tests," complained Dr. Grant.

"A racehorse is never 'just' a horse," said Mr. Barrett. "You've purchased about the most expensive bunch of high-strung nerves that was ever created."

7

A MYSTERIOUS BARN

Jody felt frightened for a moment when the back door to the horse trailer slammed shut, leaving her alone with a thousand pounds of high-strung nerves and with only a forty-five-pound dog to help her.

Dr. Connelly had wasted no time in getting his horse trailer over to the stable and loading Pure Energy into his van. It was almost as if he didn't want Mr. Barrett to have a chance to change his mind. Dr. Grant had left in a huff, saying that she would expect a report from Dr. Connelly on Pure Energy's condition as soon as possible.

Very little light came through the small opening at the top of the trailer. Jody checked the lead lines tying Pure Energy to the horse box. Peter and Mr. Barrett had both warned her that a loose horse was very dangerous. If the van had to make

41

any sharp turns, Pure Energy could fall and break his leg. The lines had to be loose, but not so loose that Pure Energy could get himself tangled up.

"You seem to be in good spirits," said Jody, "for a horse who just lost his first race in America." Pure Energy nuzzled her arm, and Jody could feel his warm breath on her neck. "Well, even if you never win a race," she whispered, "I think you're the greatest, and you deserve good grades for changing your disposition."

Jody sat down on the straw. She must have been much more tired than she realized for, before she knew it, she was being shaken awake, almost roughly.

For a second she couldn't remember exactly where she was. Then she felt the straw underneath her. Dr. Connelly was standing over her. "Jody . . . Jody," he was calling. Jody shook herself awake.

"I'm sorry . . . I must have fallen asleep."

"You were sound asleep. I think the racetrack hours must be catching up with you."

"They are," agreed Jody. "I hate to get up in the morning. Are we there yet?"

"Yes, it's time to get Pure Energy out of the van. I thought it would be better if you lead him out."

Jody stood up. She was covered with hay. "I must look like a scarecrow," she said self-consciously.

"You look too pretty to be a scarecrow," said

Dr. Connelly gallantly. "You wouldn't scare off any crows."

Jody blushed. She wiped as many straws as she could out of her hair. Pure Energy seemed extremely calm over on his side of the box. He followed Jody out with no trouble.

Dr. Connelly's office complex was quite elaborate. He had a beautiful brick home and a separate smaller building for his office. Set off to the side were several small barns where animals could be kept in isolation.

"I'll just take Pure Energy to our receiving barn," said Dr. Connelly. "You can go up to the house, and my wife will give you some lemonade."

"I'll help you get Pure Energy settled," said Jody.

"No, it's all right," said Dr. Connelly kindly. "You're tired. You've had a hard day. After all, you're not used to racecourse life. I'll see to him."

"How long do you think you'll have to keep him for your tests?" Jody asked.

"Oh, a day or two," said Dr. Connelly. "It shouldn't be much more than that."

Dr. Connelly pulled on Pure Energy's lead line, but Pure Energy shook his head furiously. Suddenly, Pure Energy reared in the air, and Dr. Connelly violently yanked on his reins. Pure Energy reared again, and the reins came flying out of Dr. Connelly's hands. Jody heard him curse violently.

"Pure Energy!" she cried.

Pure Energy looked around at his new surroundings; he seemed totally confused and a little panicked. He galloped full speed for ten yards and then looked around and switched directions.

"Stop him!" shouted Dr. Connelly. But his voice sounded so shrill that Pure Energy only panicked more.

"Easy, Pure Energy, easy," Jody crooned. Pure Energy ran toward the outbuildings down the hill from the main receiving barn. A horse stabled in one of the buildings seemed to sense something was wrong and it gave a loud whinny.

Jody ran after Pure Energy, hoping to block him off. She managed to get in front of him and stood blocking his path with her arms outstretched. Only as he came closer did she realize this was a stupid thing to do. Pure Energy could knock a ninety-eight-pound girl out of the way with a mere flick of his mane.

Just as she was about to jump to safety, Pure Energy suddenly came to a halt. He began pacing in circles, the circles getting tighter and tighter. He flared his nostrils and shook his head nervously.

Talking softly the whole time, Jody moved closer and grabbed his lead lines. Meanwhile, she could hear the horse in the small barn thrashing at his stall.

"Good work," said Dr. Connelly, running up

to her, out of breath. "I can see you can't leave this rogue alone for a minute, or he'll take advantage of you."

"He's not a rogue," said Jody defensively. "He was when Mr. Barrett first started to train him, but in just two weeks he's calmed down."

"He certainly doesn't act calmed down," said Dr. Connelly. Jody watched Dr. Connelly brusquely lead Pure Energy away. He handed the horse to his assistant. Jody wanted to say that Pure Energy didn't take to being yanked around, but Dr. Connelly had years more experience than she did, and besides, everyone at the racetrack said he was one of the best veterinarians in the business.

"I'll meet you up at the house," said Dr. Connelly. "I just have to check a few things and make sure all the animals are fed."

Jody thought he must be a very conscientious vet if he even checked on the animals' feed. She watched him walk down toward the outbuildings.

She walked up the hill toward Dr. Connelly's house. She decided that a glass of lemonade would taste wonderful. She had taken only a few steps when a horse in one of the outbuildings whinnied again. He sounded very upset. Jody could hear him banging against the walls of his stall.

He sounds like he's in a rage, Jody said to herself. Then she laughed at herself for assuming the horse was a he. *He could be a mare,* Jody thought to herself. In fact, she knew that many breeders send their mares with foal to the vet's in order to ensure a safe delivery.

The horse banged against its stall again and neighed even louder.

I wonder if Dr. Connelly needs help, thought Jody. She looked around to see if any of Dr. Connelly's assistants were in sight. She couldn't see anybody.

I think I'll just go see, Jody thought to herself. To her surprise, the door to the small barn was shut with a large combination lock. Usually, buildings around the racetrack, like stables, were open since so many people had to go in and out, feeding the horses four times a day, getting them out for exercise, cleaning their stalls.

It must be an awfully valuable horse, thought Jody. She circled the barn. It was really tiny— probably had room for just one horse. There was a small upper level, used for storing bales of hay. Jody thought she heard something moving in the hayloft.

"Dr. Connelly?" she shouted, wondering if he was up there.

There was no answer. Jody found a small window in the back; she climbed onto a bale of hay on the ground and peered through. She caught a glimpse of a dark chestnut horse in a corner.

Suddenly, she felt a rush of air from above, and

46

something heavy and hard hit her on the top of her head. She sank to her knees and threw her hands out in front of herself to break her fall. The last thing she remembered before she blacked out was the sight of a frightened chestnut horse staring at her through the window.

8

ACCIDENTS DO HAPPEN

Jody felt something cool and damp on her forehead. She felt a sharp pain in the back of her head and for several seconds she just didn't have the energy to open her eyes. But she could feel that she was lying on something soft. A feather quilt was tucked around her shoulders.

"I think she's coming around," she heard a female voice say, "but I still think we should call the ambulance."

"You're right," said a male voice. "I'll call them."

Jody summoned up the strength to open her eyes. For a second everything seemed fuzzy, and then her vision cleared. She saw a woman she had never seen before hovering near her, a very concerned look on her face.

"She's awake," said the woman. She rested a

hand on Jody's shoulder. "You're all right, dear. Don't try to move."

Dr. Connelly's face appeared. "Jody?" he asked gently. "Are you all right?"

"I think so," whispered Jody in a voice so soft that even she could hardly hear it. Jody tried to sit up, but the pain in the back of her head was so sharp that she lay right back down again.

She rested with her eyes closed for a couple of seconds. "What happened to me?" Jody asked, opening her eyes again.

"That's what I was hoping you could tell us," said Dr. Connelly.

"I don't remember anything," murmured Jody.

"I found you down by the barn," said Dr. Connelly. "It looked as if a bale of hay from the loft had fallen on you."

"I've been wanting you to fix that hayloft for the longest time," said Mrs. Connelly sharply. "Now maybe you'll listen to me."

"I'm okay," said Jody. "It's funny. It didn't feel like a bale of hay." She sat up and looked around. The Connellys' living room was one of the prettiest rooms Jody had ever seen. Many different styles of old furniture somehow seemed to mesh together. In the bookcase by the wall, books with beautiful leather bindings seemed carefully arranged.

Dr. Connelly reached over and felt Jody's head. His hands probed very gently to see if the skin was broken. "You're definitely going to have a lump," he said.

"Shouldn't she be checked to see if she has a concussion?" asked Mrs. Connelly. She still sounded terribly anxious.

"It would probably be a good idea," said Dr. Connelly. "After all, I'm a horse doctor, not a people doctor; but Jody seems like a strong girl."

"Honestly," said Jody, "I feel okay. My head hurts. I just wish I could remember better how it happened. Somehow, a bale of hay seems all wrong."

"Well, certainly a bale of hay on your head would feel all wrong," said Dr. Connelly, laughing.

Jody gave a half-hearted laugh in agreement. She rubbed the top of her head. It felt sore, but not too tender to the touch.

Just then the doorbell rang. "I'll get it," said Mrs. Connelly. Left alone with Dr. Connelly, Jody felt uncomfortable. She thought he felt guilty that she had gotten hurt on his premises because he kept staring at her with such a worried expression.

"Honestly, Dr. Connelly," she said reassuringly, "I'm fine."

"Well, accidents do happen," said Dr. Connelly. "It's just that I feel responsible."

"I could tell," said Jody, "but it wasn't your fault."

Dr. Connelly looked relieved.

I wonder if he thought I was going to sue him because he knows Mom's a lawyer, Jody thought to herself. Jody heard footsteps rushing through the hall. Jake came running into the room with Peter close behind him.

"Jody! Are you all right? Mrs. Connelly just told us you got knocked out." Jake sounded anxious.

"I'm fine," said Jody, feeling a little embarrassed by all the fuss.

"How did it happen?" asked Peter.

"I don't know," said Jody, but Peter couldn't hear her answer because at the same time Dr. Connelly spoke loudly.

"She got hit on the head with a loose bale of hay. It fell from our hayloft."

"Ouch!" winced Peter. "They weigh thirty pounds when they're packed tight."

"I always knew you had a hard head," said Jake, "but you didn't need to prove it."

Jody smiled weakly. She could tell from the tone of Jake's voice that he was really worried. "I'm fine," she repeated. "The Connellys have been taking good care of me. Let's go home."

She got to her feet. For a second, her knees felt like they might buckle under her. She leaned against the sofa armrest for support.

"Jody!" said Jake, running to her side. "You don't look like you're all right."

"I am!" Jody insisted.

"You can stay here for a while," Dr. Connelly said. "Perhaps we should call your mother."

"No. Peter and Jake can take me home," said Jody. "Honestly, I'm fine."

"If you're so fine, how come you look green," said Jake. "You look a little like a frog."

"Well, I'm not about to croak," said Jody, making a froglike sound deep in her throat.

"Now I know you got hit on the head," said Jake. "You're making puns."

"We'd better get her to the hospital right away," said Peter.

"Seriously," warned Dr. Connelly, "if you feel at all nauseated, or if you have a headache after today, you must promise me to go to a hospital. You could have a concussion and not know about it yet."

"Yeah," said Jake, "Jody often doesn't know what happened to her until after it's happened."

"Shut up, Jake," said Peter. He looked terribly worried. "Come on, Jody," he said softly, "I'll take you home."

Peter put his arm around Jody's waist. "I *am* fine," she whispered, but she felt steadier with Peter's arm around her.

Dr. and Mrs. Connelly followed them to the car. "Will you please call us and let us know how you feel tomorrow?" asked Dr. Connelly.

"I will," said Jody, "but please stop worrying, everybody."

Peter settled Jody in the front seat. "Let me get

a blanket from the back to put around you," he said. He reached ino the back seat and pulled out an old horse blanket.

"It stinks," said Jody, but she was glad for its warmth. Whether from shock or fear, she found herself shivering. "Let's get out of here," she muttered, "please."

Peter turned and stared at her. Jody's voice sounded strangely urgent for someone who had just been insisting that she was fine.

9

JUST A LITTLE
CLUNK ON
THE HEAD

"Wow!" said Jake from the back seat as they drove out of Dr. Connelly's driveway. "He's got quite a spread for a veterinarian."

"A lot of the vets do very well around the race-track," said Peter. "Sometimes a lot better than the trainers. They're not as dependent on the whims of owners." Peter turned back to Jody. "Are you really all right?" he asked.

"I think I've heard that question enough for today," she said. "Seriously, Peter, I'm fine. It was a little clunk on the head. I bet I wasn't unconscious for more than two or three minutes."

"Why, I've seen you when you've been unconscious for days," said Jake, "only you fooled the rest of the world."

"Very funny," said Jody. "You know what was funny?"

"You're joke about croaking?" said Jake. "That was pretty funny, but I wouldn't put it in the Joke Hall of Fame."

"I'm being serious," said Jody.

"Now I know you're back to normal," said Jake.

"Stop teasing her," said Peter, "and let her talk."

"Thanks," said Jody glancing over at Peter. His eyes were on the road and both hands on the wheel, but he still had that look of concern on his face.

"I can't believe that it was a bale of hay that fell on me," said Jody. "I had the distinct impression right before I blacked out that somebody was behind me."

"Maybe it was somebody dressed up as a bale of hay," said Jake. Peter turned to the back and gave Jake a dirty look.

"Don't mind him," said Jody.

"I don't," admitted Peter. "Why would somebody hit you on the head?"

"I don't know," said Jody. "I suppose it could have been a prowler."

"Why would somebody want to steal something out of Dr. Connelly's barn?" asked Jake. "Now his house is another matter. That's a pretty fancy place."

"Yeah," said Peter, "I remember somebody telling me that Doc Connelly collected rare books about horses. He's supposed to have one of the best collections in the country."

"Somehow, I can't see a rare-book thief hitting Jody over the head," said Jake.

"Me either," said Jody. "Listen, maybe I'm just making a mountain out of a molehill."

"Why did the mountain stop smoking?" asked Jake.

"Why?" asked Peter.

"Because he knew it made the mole ill," said Jake.

Jody groaned. "This is worse than getting hit over the head."

"See," said Jake, "I knew I could take your mind off your troubles."

"Come on, Jake, be serious," said Peter. "If Jody thinks somebody deliberately hit her over the head, it's no joking matter."

"I'm not really sure," said Jody. "Maybe it could have been a bale of hay. Dr. Connelly was pretty sure that's what caused it."

"Yeah, but he wasn't actually there when you were knocked out, was he?" asked Jake.

"No," said Jody. "At least I don't think so. He said he found me down by the barn."

"Were you putting Pure Energy down there?" asked Jake.

"No," said Jody. "Dr. Connelly took Pure Energy. Now it's coming back to me. Pure Energy got loose and there was another horse in that barn that was making a big fuss, so I went to see if he was in trouble."

"Pure Energy got loose?" said Peter, his voice almost cracking.

"Oh, no. Dr. Connelly and I caught him again. He was loose for only a few minutes."

"Whew!" said Peter. "For a second I thought Dad was going to have to explain to that Dr. Grant that we lost her horse."

"She's a tough lady," said Jake. "She's not exactly easy to work for."

"You can say that again," said Peter. "She certainly seemed to think it was my fault that Pure Energy lost."

"Anybody could see that he just didn't have it in him to win that race," said Jody. "Gosh, it seems like that race was days ago."

"That's because you were knocked out," said Peter. "That's happened to me when I've taken a fall and been unconscious, even for just a few minutes. It always feels as if you've lost days."

"You make it sound as if being knocked out is an average occurrence," said Jake.

"Well, it does happen a lot around the racetrack," said Peter. "Accidents are always happening."

"You'd better come in and explain that to our Mom," said Jake as they pulled into the Marksons' driveway.

"I'll help Jody in," said Peter. He slipped out of

the driver's seat and walked around to open Jody's door. He started to pick her up.

"I'm not an invalid," said Jody. "Come on. You'll scare Mom to death if you carry me inside."

"What is going to scare me to death?" asked Mrs. Markson, suddenly appearing from around the side of the house. "Jody, what's wrong?" she asked anxiously.

"How can you tell anything's wrong?" demanded Jody.

"You look pale," said Mrs. Markson. "Did you fall off a horse?"

"No, Mom, I'm okay," said Jody.

"She was just knocked out for a couple of minutes, Mrs. Markson," Peter explained.

"Knocked out!" cried Mrs. Markson.

"Mom, I'm fine. Apparently, a bale of hay fell on me at the vet's. Or . . ." Jody's voice trailed off.

Mrs. Markson helped Jody into the house and settled her on the couch. "I'm calling the doctor and having her check you over," said Mrs. Markson.

The Marksons' cats, Groucho and Chico, curled up at Jody's feet. "Everybody doesn't have to make such a fuss," said Jody. "Peter gets knocked out all the time."

Mrs. Markson stared at Peter, horrified. "That's not exactly true," said Peter, "but I was just telling Jody that it's happened to me."

"I'm not sure I want you working at the racetrack," said Mrs. Markson. "First you came home with that black-and-blue mark when Pure Energy bit you, and now this."

"Well, at least it's never boring," said Jake. Mrs. Markson went out to call the doctor.

"Jake," Jody whispered, "don't tell Mom that I think it might have been a person who did it. Promise?"

"I won't," said Jake. "But Jody, if you really think it wasn't an accident, we should tell somebody."

"I know," said Jody, "but I don't want to make a big deal about it. I could have been wrong and I don't want Mom to get any more upset than she is. I'd hate it if she wanted us to quit our jobs."

"I'd hate it too," said Peter. "Dad and I have really come to depend on you two. Dad says that you're the best thing to happen to our stable in a long time."

"Thanks," said Jody. "I'm glad that somebody doesn't think I'm accident prone."

"Okay," said Jake, "I'll keep quiet. Only just don't go around getting knocked on the head anymore."

"Don't worry," said Jody, "I don't plan on it."

10
DON'T EXPECT MIRACLES

"Pure Energy's coming back tomorrow," Jody said excitedly at dinner about a week later.

"I didn't realize he had been away," said Mrs. Markson dryly.

"He's been at Dr. Connelly's all this time," said Jody impatiently. "I really miss him."

"I don't know," said Mrs. Markson. "Since he's been away you haven't been bitten on the arm or knocked over the head. I've gotten used to your coming home in one piece."

"Oh, Mom," said Jody, "Pure Energy wasn't to blame. I told you, accidents are just part of the game at the track."

"Yeah," said Jake, "like losing your shirt. You'd be surprised how many shirts turn up at the lost-and-found at the racetrack."

"You haven't been losing your shirt, have you?" asked Mrs. Markson sharply.

"Me?" said Jake, innocently. "It's illegal for minors to bet. Besides, I don't bet real money. Mr. Barrett says that anybody who really thinks you can beat the races is just plain stupid. He says that you can win a race, but nobody beats the races."

"He sounds like a smart man," said Mrs. Markson. "I like Mr. Barrett. Has he really recovered from his heart attack?"

"I think so," said Jody. "Things seem much more calm now."

"Well, let's hope they stay that way once you get that horse back."

"I don't see what you have against Pure Energy," complained Jody.

"Well, I don't like horses that bite my daughter," said Mrs. Markson. "You can just call me prejudiced."

Jody laughed.

The next morning Jody woke up at 5:25, five minutes before her alarm went off. She grinned to herself. She loved her work at the racetrack so much she was actually enjoying getting up early.

She got into the bathroom before Jake. Several minutes later, Jake rattled the doorknob in disbelief that somebody had gotten in before him.

"Who's there?" he demanded.

"Me," mumbled Jody with her toothbrush in her mouth.

"Me, who?" asked Jake. "Is that my sister or a burglar?"

"What burglar would answer 'me'?" shouted Jody.

"I don't know," said Jake. "If you talked to him politely, he might answer you."

"Go away, Jake," said Jody. "I'm going to wash my hair."

"What are you doing up this early? And why are you in such a talkative mood? You don't usually talk in the morning."

"I know," said Jody. "I just woke up in a good mood."

"Well, hurry up in there," said Jake. "I think I might prefer the grouchy Jody better—the one who lets me in the bathroom first."

Jody just ignored him. When Mr. Barrett and Peter honked to pick them up, Jody ran out to the car, but Harpo beat her and jumped into the back seat. Peter smiled at her.

When they got to the track Buster waved at them. "Beautiful morning," he said. "I got a hot tip on the sixth."

"Oh, Buster," said Mr. Barrett, "how much money have you lost over the years on hot tips."

Buster looked a little embarrassed. Then he brightened up. "Who's counting? Besides, one winner can make up for a lot of losers."

Mr. Barrett just shook his head. "Well, good luck, Buster."

"Good luck!" Jody yelled. Buster gave her a big smile. "Thank you, lassy. Maybe you'll bring me luck today."

"Poor Buster," said Mr. Barrett. "He's always got a hot tip, but he's never got a dime."

"Don't you ever bet?" Jake asked. "Even on your own horse—one you've trained?"

"Almost never," said Mr. Barrett. "That's why I've saved enough money to send Peter to college."

Peter made a face, but Mr. Barrett ignored him.

As they were walking to the stable, Peter caught up with Jody. "You do look terrific today," he said.

"Thanks," said Jody, and she blushed. Lately, she and Peter had been spending more and more time together, and Jody did not quite know what to think about it. She just knew that she liked getting up and going to work better and better each day. Yet if she thought about liking Peter seriously she got all tongue-tied and awkward-feeling. It was much easier just to talk about horses.

"Do you think Pure Energy will remember me?" Jody asked.

"Sure. He's the type of horse that never forgets a pretty face," said Peter, grinning. "Come to think of it, maybe that explains why he runs so slow."

"What are you talking about?" asked Jake, coming up beside them.

"I decided Pure Energy runs so slow because he's always trying to pick out the pretty girls in the crowd. If he ran fast, he knows he'd miss them."

"You're an idiot," said Jody. "Besides, who knows? Maybe Dr. Connelly has him all fixed up and he's going to be a winner."

"If he could do that to Pure Energy, he'd be put in jail," joked Peter. "The only thing that would turn that horse into a winner would be a whole transplant."

"You wait and see," said Jody.

Dr. Connelly was waiting at the stables with Dr. Grant. He held Pure Energy on a lead line. "Here he is, as good as new," he said. "He had an intestinal problem, but it's cleared up."

"He wasn't acting like he had an intestinal bug," said Mr. Barrett. "It's funny. He was way off his feed when I first got him, but he was eating good right at the end."

"Well, the tests showed up positive," said Dr. Connelly, speaking quickly. "I have him on antibiotics, but I think you can take him off them now. He should be in good shape."

"That's good," said Dr. Grant, "because I want to enter him in the $100,000 Gold Cup Stakes next month."

"But the entry fee is over $10,000," insisted Mr. Barrett. "You'd be foolish to throw that money away. Let me enter him in a few other races where he won't be outclassed."

"I can't understand your attitude," complained Dr. Grant. "You act as if you don't want my horse to win."

"But Dr. Grant, of course I want Pure Energy to win. It's just that some of the best horses in the country will be running in the Gold Cup. Pure Energy won't be able to keep up. You can ruin a horse's spirit that way. Isn't that right, Doc?"

"Well," hesitated Dr. Connelly, clearly not wanting to get into the middle. "It may be that after his rest, Pure Energy will do much better."

Mr. Barrett sighed. "Dr. Grant, it's your money. If you want to enter him in the Gold Cup, I'll do what I can to get him ready. Just don't expect miracles."

11
ACCIDENT PRONE?

Jody watched Peter take Pure Energy around the track. Mr. Barrett held a stopwatch. He stared at the stopwatch in disbelief.

"I wonder if it's broken," he asked.

"Why?" said Jody.

"He just did that quarter mile at an incredible speed," said Mr. Barrett. "I hope Peter isn't pushing him too hard."

Jody looked back at Peter. Peter was standing in the stirrups, holding Pure Energy back. He rode absolutely balanced. He seemed so firmly centered, you could balance a full glass of water on his back without spilling a drop.

Peter slowed Pure Energy down and came alongside Jody and Mr. Barrett at the rail.

"Did you use the whip?" asked Mr. Barrett.

"No, Dad," said Peter in surprise. "I didn't have to touch him once. He just had a lot of speed."

"Are you sure you weren't driving him?" insisted Mr. Barrett. "It doesn't make sense that he should have been going so fast."

"I know, Dad," said Peter. "It surprised me too. Maybe he's just feeling good today. He even seemed to have a lot of speed left over."

Mr. Barrett ran his hand along Pure Energy's flank. "He hasn't even worked up much of a sweat," he said.

Peter grinned. "Who knows?" he said. "Maybe that crazy Dr. Grant knew what she was doing when she entered him in the Gold Cup."

"Now, don't you get your hopes up," warned Mr. Barrett. "And don't go talking to anybody else about how much faster he seems. We don't want any rumors flying about this horse."

Peter winked at Jody. "No spreading any hot tips."

"I'm serious," said Mr. Barrett.

"I know, Dad," said Peter. "I'm sorry. It's just that I still can't believe that Pure Energy would ever have the stuff to really finish in the money."

"Neither can I, son," said Mr. Barrett. "Neither can I."

Peter hopped off Pure Energy and handed him to Jody. "Can you take him back to the stables for me?" he asked. "I'm supposed to gallop another horse in five minutes."

"Sure," said Jody. She started to lead Pure

Energy back to the stables. Harpo came bounding up to her, wagging his tail. Suddenly, without any warning, Pure Energy lashed out with his back hoof. His razor-sharp horseshoes narrowly missed Harpo's head.

"Pure Energy!" shouted Jody. "Stop that!" Pure Energy's ears were laid back and his lips curled up over his teeth.

"What's wrong, Jody?" shouted Peter, running up.

"He just tried to kick Harpo," said Jody. "I can't believe it. Normally, they're best friends."

Harpo was cowering to the side, his tail between his legs. Peter went over and patted Harpo on the head. "Hey, boy. Don't be scared. Maybe Pure Energy is just feeling his oats after such a good run." Peter looked up and saw the worried look on Jody's face.

"Hey, don't take it so seriously," he said lightly. "Horses are unpredictable."

"Well, it was so unexpected, it scared me," said Jody.

"Don't worry about it," said Peter, preoccupied with thinking about the next horse he had to ride. "Take him back. I'll see you at the stables."

Jody walked Pure Energy back. She had a hard time controlling him. He seemed to be feeling so good he could hardly contain himself. He pranced around with the proud, challenging gait of a winner. Harpo kept a respectful distance.

At the stables, Dr. Connelly was waiting. He

was holding another chestnut horse all saddled up. "How did he do today?" he asked.

"Pretty good," said Jody, careful not to commit herself. She remembered Mr. Barrett's warning about not spreading rumors. She liked Dr. Connelly, but she remembered his reputation as a gossip.

"How are you feeling?" he asked. "You aren't having any headaches after that little accident, are you?"

"No," said Jody. "I've been feeling just fine."

"Why don't you let me cool him down. You can do your other chores."

"No, it's okay," said Jody.

"Seriously," said Dr. Connelly. "I have to wait here. I want to talk to Jared about something. You could do me a favor. Could you ride this horse over to the receiving barn? I promised the vet over there that he could have a look at him."

"Well," said Jody, "I don't know. Mr. Barrett had a lot for me to do."

"I'll explain to him that you were doing a favor for me," said Dr. Connelly. "Here, let me give you a leg up."

"Well, all right," said Jody, not wanting to be disagreeable. She mounted the horse. He seemed like a calm animal, but he was very tall for a racehorse.

She swung the horse around to head for the receiving barn when, suddenly, she felt the saddle slipping beneath her.

"What the . . . ?" she shouted, trying to keep her balance.

The saddle now had practically completely slipped around the horse's stomach. Jody tried to scramble back up, but she lost hold of the reins. She held on to his mane and tried to keep her balance, but she couldn't do it. She felt herself slipping and it seemed like the ground rushed up to meet her.

She landed with a loud thud and rolled out of the way of the horse's hooves. She sprang up to her feet and grabbed the horse's reins just as Mr. Barrett and Peter were walking back to the stable.

"What happened?" shouted Mr. Barrett, rushing to her side. Dr. Connelly stood next to Pure Energy, trying to keep him calm.

"It's nothing," said Jody. "I was just taking this horse over to the receiving barn for Dr. Connelly, and the saddle was loose."

"Are you okay?" asked Peter.

"Yeah," said Jody, looking down at herself. She was covered with dirt. "It was just an accident. The girth must not have been tightened."

"It was fine when I was riding him," said Dr. Connelly. Jody stared at him. He seemed to be suggesting that somehow the accident had been her fault.

"There have been too many accidents around here lately," said Mr. Barrett.

"But—but . . ." stammered Jody, "people fall

off and have accidents all the time. It wasn't my fault."

"I just don't want you hurt," said Mr. Barrett.

"I'm fine!" said Jody angrily.

"Cool it, Jody," whispered Peter. "My Dad's just upset. He hates to see anybody hurt around his stable. He's always had one of the best safety records at the track. Come on. I'll help you take Dr. Connelly's horse over to the receiving barn."

As they left, Jody saw Mr. Barrett deep in conversation with Dr. Connelly. They kept stealing glances at her, and it made Jody feel very uncomfortable.

Walking to the receiving barn with Peter, she kept protesting that the accident hadn't been her fault. "The saddle just slipped out from under me," said Jody. "It must have been loose before."

"Well, Doc Connelly's a big man," said Peter. "He might have loosened it. Don't worry about it."

Jody kept quiet. She couldn't put into words exactly what she felt, almost as if events were ganging up on her, trying to make her feel incompetent, like someone who couldn't quite handle herself around a racetrack.

When they got back to the stables, Jody's worst fears came true. Dr. Connelly had gone, but Mr. Barrett seemed to be waiting for her. "Jody, there's something I want to talk to you about," he said.

Jody felt her heart start to beat very fast. She

just nodded her head. Mrs. Markson always joked that the nine most frightening words in the English language were, "There's something I want to talk to you about." Listening to them now, Jody knew she was right.

"Jody, I know you're a hard worker," began Mr. Barrett. Jody knew from the tone of his voice that there was a big "but" coming soon. She was right.

"But," continued Mr. Barrett, "some people are just accident prone. I know. I've seen it around the track before. I like you. I know you're smart and you care about horses. But Dr. Connelly and I were talking, and for your own good, I think it would be best if you didn't work here anymore. I wouldn't want to see you seriously hurt."

Jody felt tears well up in her eyes and she shook her head fiercely to make herself stop crying. She felt Peter almost unconsciously take her hand, as if to steady her.

"But I'm not accident prone," she objected. "You can ask my mom, Jake, anybody. It's just been one of those freak coincidences. And it's only a couple accidents, anyway. You can't condemn a person just because of a few accidents."

"Jody, Jody," sighed Mr. Barrett. "I'm not condemning you. I'm only thinking of your own good. I would never forgive myself if you got hurt while working for me. And frankly, Dr. Connelly mentioned that he didn't think it was good for my heart to have an added worry. I'm afraid he's right. I want to be fair. I'll pay you two weeks severance pay."

"Dad," protested Peter, "you *are not* being fair. You can't fire Jody just because of a few dumb accidents. Look at all the times I've fallen off horses or had accidents. They happen around the track. You can't be around horses all the time and not have accidents. But Jody has taken good care of herself."

"Peter, I've made up my mind about this," said Mr. Barrett. "Dr. Connelly and I agree that for Jody's own good she shouldn't be put into a position where she might hurt herself."

Jody no longer felt like crying. Now she was furious. It was so unfair, but she knew that nothing she could say would change Mr. Barrett's mind.

12
I WISH YOU LUCK

Jody couldn't believe she had been fired. She knew deep in her heart that she was *not* accident prone, but it was a label that seemed impossible to disprove. Peter had argued and argued with his father, but Mr. Barrett had refused to budge. Jody felt as if she had turned into a symbol of bad luck for Mr. Barrett.

Mrs. Markson had been sympathetic when Jody told her what had happened, but she seemed to feel that Mr. Barrett had a point. "You can't blame him for worrying about you," she said. "First you were bitten on the arm, and then you were knocked out. He does have some good evidence that you've had your share of accidents. Besides, Mr. Barrett himself is just recovering from a heart attack. He doesn't need any outside worries."

A week went by. Every morning Jody still woke up early. She would hear Jake get up and leave the house, and every time she heard Jake go, she felt awful.

Jody rolled over in her bed and looked at her clock. The alarm button was pushed in, but still she was awake. 5:45 A.M. At least today, Jody knew she would be returning to the track. Today, Peter was riding Pure Energy in the Gold Cup. Mrs. Markson had agreed to go to the track with Jody.

Jody heard Jake moving around. She thought she heard a soft knock on the back door. She looked out the window. No strange car had driven up. A few seconds later, Jody definitely heard a knock on her own door.

"Jody," Jake whispered, "are you awake?"

"Jody slipped on her robe and went to the door. "Yeah," she said. "What's up?"

"Peter wanted you to wish him luck this morning. He's downstairs. He walked over early this morning."

"Oh!" said Jody so softly Jake hardly could hear her.

" 'Oh'? Is that all you have to say?" said Jake. "The guy got up at five in the morning to come see you. I happen to know that Peter likes getting up early about as much as you do."

"I'm not sure I should see him," said Jody. "Maybe I'll bring him bad luck."

Jake gave her a disgusted look. "Would you stop this moping around? You've been about as much fun as a pet rock lately, and Peter has been too. You'd better get down there, or I'll pick you up and carry you myself."

"Well, just let me wash my face. Tell him I'll be down in a minute."

"You'd better make that a literal minute," said Jake.

Jody quickly ran a brush through her hair. She glanced at herself in the mirror. To her surprise, she thought she didn't look like the Dragon Lady who brings misfortune to everyone she sees. She looked like Jody Markson, fairly tall, slim and with nice brown eyes. Even her hair looked like normal hair, not like snakes. Jody gave it one last brush and ran down the stairs, feeling happier than she had in a long time.

Peter was sitting at the kitchen table, nervously tracing the pattern on the tablecloth. He looked up when Jody came in.

"Hi," he said shyly.

"Hi," said Jody. "Are you excited about the race?"

"Yeah," said Peter. "I still think Pure Energy's outclassed. But it's very exciting to be given a chance to ride any horse in the Gold Cup."

"Well, I wish you luck," said Jody, feeling stiff and slightly awkward. She and Peter were talking to each other as if they hardly knew each other.

"How's Pure Energy doing?" Jody asked.

"He seems fine," said Peter. "I don't know what Doc Connelly did to him, but he's got a lot more energy than he used to."

"Maybe he gave him energy pills," said Jody.

"Well, I hope they were pure," said Peter. "I'm sorry. That was a pretty weak excuse for a joke."

"Yeah, it was," admitted Jody. "But it's early in the morning."

"Jody, I've been wanting to talk to you ever since my dad fired you, but I was too embarrassed. I figured you were mad at all the Barretts and wouldn't want anything to do with any of us."

"Oh, no," said Jody quickly. "I thought you figured I was bad luck and that's why you were staying away."

"No," said Peter. "I still think my dad was crazy to fire you, but he's a stubborn man and somehow he's convinced you were going to get seriously hurt."

"I'm not a piece of poreclain china that has to be kept on a shelf," protested Jody.

"I know," said Peter. He smiled at her. "Jake said you and your mom are coming to the races today."

"Yeah. We'll cheer for you."

"Just don't bet on me," said Peter. "Given Pure Energy's record, you'd just be throwing money away. Ask any handicapper."

"Well, I'll be cheering for you and Pure Energy anyhow," said Jody.

Peter got up to go. "I'm glad you're going to be there," he said, smiling.

Jody watched him leave. She felt better than she had in days. Maybe if she ran into Mr. Barrett at the track, he'd reconsider and take her back. Jody longed to go back to work at the stables. Seeing Peter had made her realize how much she missed it . . . and him.

When her mother got up a few hours later, Jody was dressed and ready to go. "You look bright-eyed and bushy-tailed today," said Mrs. Markson, staring into her cup of coffee. Mrs. Markson always said that Jody had inherited her early morning genes . . . genes that urged her body to stay in bed.

"Let's get going to the track," said Jody.

"Can I finish my cup of coffee?" said Mrs. Markson. "What's our hurry? The Gold Cup is the eighth race. I checked in the paper."

"I know," said Jody, "but it's my first time back in over a week. I want to get there."

Mrs. Markson smiled. "To get there or to see Peter?" she said, but she hurriedly took another sip of her coffee.

"Mother!" protested Jody.

Mrs. Markson immediately regretted teasing Jody, especially after she had warned Jake against doing it. "Okay, honey. I'll get ready quickly, and we'll drive to the track. I'm excited about seeing the Gold Cup myself."

When they got to the track, the parking lot was already nearly full. "It was practically empty the last time I came," said Mrs. Markson.

"That was just a regular day," said Jody. On the day of a big race, there's always a crowd. Did you know that racing is the leading spectator sport? Nearly eighty million people go to the track. That's nearly a third more than go to a baseball game; then comes football, basketball and hockey."

"You've become a regular encyclopedia about horse racing," said Mrs. Markson.

"It's a hard sport to get into," said Jody. "It looks as if it's much less complicated than baseball or football because, after all, it's just a race, but there's so many statistics to learn . . . and bloodlines. It's been like learning a whole new language."

"And you miss it since you've been fired, don't you?" said Mrs. Markson sympathetically.

"Yeah," said Jody, nodding her head. "I miss it a whole lot."

13
THE GOLD CUP

The grandstand at the racetrack was crowded for the running of the Gold Cup. Jody could feel the intense excitement as the crowds waited for the eighth race, the Gold Cup.

"I wish I could be in the stables with them," said Jody. "I've finally gotten to know Pure Energy and maybe I would bring him luck."

"Well, we'll go to that place where they parade the horses before the race. He'll be there, won't he?" asked Mrs. Markson.

"It's called the paddock, Mom," answered Jody. "Let's go now, so we can get a good place to stand."

Jake was given the job of parading Pure Energy around the paddock, the job that Jody had once had. Pure Energy seemed perfectly relaxed. In fact, Jake seemed by far the more nervous of the two.

"Boy, he's sure acting differently from the last time I saw him," said a voice behind Jody and Mrs. Markson.

"Oh, hi," said Mrs. Markson, turning to face Liz Gerber. "I was hoping I would see you today. Do you have any advice for me?"

"Well, I was going to tell you not to waste your money on Pure Energy. I put his odds at eighty-to-one. I was shocked to see him even entered in this race. But I have to admit he looks pretty good parading. He almost looks like a different horse."

"That's because Mr. Barrett's such a good trainer," said Jody.

"You're right about that," said Liz Gerber. "He's got a fine reputation for calming down a nervous horse, but he'd have to be a miracle worker to pull this one out of the hat."

"Who do you think is going to win?" asked Mrs. Markson.

"Well, the favorite, Golden Sunrise, has to be taken very seriously, but Last Act has been coming along strong, and the odds are better on him. I should know. I set them this morning."

"Do you think anybody will bet on Pure Energy?" asked Jody.

"Well, there are always some fools ready to throw their money away on a long shot."

"I think you're looking at one," said Mrs.

Markson ruefully. "I think Jody will insist I back him. At least he's somebody's favorite."

"I don't think we should bet on him," said Jody indignantly. "Even Peter told me not to waste money on him. You're supposed to bet with your head, not your heart."

"Well, I think I'll put two dollars down on Pure Energy," said Mrs. Markson, "just to bring him luck."

"Come on, Mom, don't be silly," insisted Jody. "He's way outclassed. Why Mr. Barrett didn't even want him to enter this race. He only did it because Dr. Grant insisted. I think you should bet on Last Act."

"Listen to your daughter," said Liz Gerber. "She could make a good handicapper someday."

Jody smiled.

"Are you serious?" asked Mrs. Markson. "Don't you want me to bet on Pure Energy?"

"No," said Jody stubbornly.

"Are you sure you aren't just suffering from sour grapes because Mr. Barrett fired you?" asked Mrs. Markson.

"No, Mom. Mr. Barrett and Peter and I talked about betting a lot. I bet *Mr. Barrett* isn't betting on Pure Energy."

"Well, all right," said Mrs. Markson.

Jody watched Mr. Barrett give Peter his final instructions. For a second, Jody wanted to go run to her mother and tell her to put the money on Pure Energy. *Don't be stupid,* Jody told herself.

She walked over to the rail and watched Peter take Pure Energy out to the starting gate. Once again, she was astonished and even a bit hurt about how calm Pure Energy seemed. It was as if he had flourished since she had left, and Jody had to admit that she would have liked it better if Pure Energy had missed her so much he had become even more nervous than he was when he arrived.

Peter guided Pure Energy into the gate with very little trouble. In fact, it was the favorite, Golden Sunrise, who gave his rider a little trouble going into the gate. However, within seconds, all the horses were settled.

When all the horses and riders were facing in the right direction and looked ready, the official starter pushed the button that trips the latch that opens all the starting gates at once.

Pure Energy was a second off-balance coming out of the gate. He was seventh at the first turn. Golden Sunrise broke fast, but his jockey tried to restrain him. Jody could see her pulling back on the reins and settling her weight down on the saddle, trying to slow the horse down so that he'd have something for the finish. Last Act also was being held back.

Peter saw a hole toward the outside and he steered Pure Energy toward it. Pure Energy responded with a burst of speed and power.

At the top of the stretch Pure Energy had moved into third place. "Too fast, too fast," muttered Jody, more to herself than to anybody else. "He'll never be able to hold out."

Now Golden Sunrise and Last Act were ready to make their moves. They inched up on Pure Energy, but miraculously, when Peter asked Pure Energy for more speed, he stretched his legs out even further in a huge, driving move.

With a little more than half a mile remaining in the race, Pure Energy and Peter took charge. Inch by inch, Peter lowered his slim body over Pure Energy and moved the reins forward to ask for even more speed. The gesture was so smooth that almost no one in the crowd except Jody noticed. But Pure Energy noticed. Suddenly, he sprinted away from Golden Sunrise and opened up a clear lead.

Far behind, Golden Sunrise was floundering. But Last Act had plenty of energy left. He took up the chase of Pure Energy, expecting to catch him in the backstretch. But Pure Energy didn't falter. Peter drove Pure Energy coolly through the stretch, urging him with his hands. Last Act moved up and pressed him, but every time he came close, Peter asked for a little more from Pure Energy, and Pure Energy gave.

Jody clutched the rail so tightly that her knuckles turned white. All around her she could hear the crowds cheering, but she felt as if she were in a cocoon, wrapped up in Peter and Pure Energy's drive toward the finish line.

Last Act's jockey was whipping his horse, ask-

ing for that last ounce of effort to catch Pure
Energy. Last Act made a gallant try, but Pure
Energy just couldn't be stopped. It was almost as
if he knew there was a horse behind him and he
was going to refuse to let it beat him. Pure Energy crossed the finish line a full length ahead of
Last Act.

Jody felt someone pounding her back. It was
Jake. Gradually, she came out of her trance. "He
won! He won!" she cried.

"Come on," said Jake, "let's go to the winner's
circle." They pushed their way through the
crowds. Mr. Barrett stood beside Dr. Grant. Dr.
Grant looked elated, but Mr. Barrett looked as
if he were in shock.

"I hope the good news isn't too much for him,"
whispered Mrs. Markson. "He looks pasty-faced."

"Come on, Mom," said Jake cheerfully, "good
luck never hurt anybody."

14

"I'M GOING
TO NEED
A LAWYER"

In honor of Pure Energy's victory, Mr. Barrett arranged for the horses to be taken care of by another trainer. He gave both Peter and Jake a day off and even planned a day off for himself.

"It's my first day off in weeks," announced Jake the next morning. "I'm making blueberry pancakes. I invited Peter and Mr. Barrett for breakfast."

"There goes my diet," announced Mrs. Markson.

"Who cares?" announced Jake. "We deserve to celebrate. A win like that will keep Mr. Barrett's stable in clover for a long time. Other owners will flock back to him like homing pigeons."

"Come on, Mom," agreed Jody, "let's break out the champagne."

"Well," said Mrs. Markson, "I'd like to remind you that it was *you* who talked me out of betting on Pure Energy."

"Come on, Mom, no sour grapes," insisted Jake. "I want only the bubbly kind."

"Number one, you're both underage, and number two . . ." Finally, Mrs. Markson burst out laughing. "You're right. Just because we didn't win is no reason not to celebrate with Peter and Mr. Barrett. I'll go put some champagne on ice. This is Mr. Barrett's day to celebrate."

"Great! I'll help Jake make the pancakes," said Jody.

"No dice," said Jake. "I want them to be delicious. You can set the table. You're a great table-setter and a lousy cook."

"I am not!" Jody started to protest, automatically, and then she realized that Jake was right. He was the better cook.

"I'm going to get some fresh flowers for the table," said Jody. "Come on, Harpo, you can come outside with me."

Harpo wagged his tail furiously at the mention of his name.

Jody was concentrating on flowers when, suddenly, a movement behind her made her jump.

Peter stood behind her, grinning.

Jody smiled up at him. "Congratulations! There were so many people around you yesterday I really didn't get a chance to congratulate you."

"Thanks," said Peter. "It was the most exciting

day of my life. I couldn't believe it. Every time I asked Pure Energy for more, he had it to give. It was like riding a dream horse."

"A little bit different from your last race on him."

"I'll say!" said Peter ."Oh, Jody, it was terrific. And as soon as things calm down, I'm going to insist that Dad rehire you. He can't bellyache about his bad luck now. Not after this win."

"How's your dad taking it?" asked Jody. "Mom was worried about him in the winner's circle. She was afraid that the excitement would be too much for him."

"Well, he should be on cloud nine," said Peter. "Did you know that he bet $500 on Pure Energy. That means he won $40,000! Not to mention that we got the traditional ten percent of the purse—which in this case was $10,000!"

Jody stared at Peter. "He bet $500!" she screeched. "And *I* talked Mom out of betting on him."

Peter laughed. "Well, Pure Energy turned out to be wonderful. Some horses do change very suddenly. It's almost as if they decide they really do want to be a racehorse. Pure Energy just ran like the wind. He refused to give up." Peter was so excited he picked Jody up and started twirling her around the garden.

"Peter!" shouted a voice sharply. Mr. Barrett stood in the driveway looking at Peter and Jody and frowning.

"We were just celebrating Pure Energy's win," said Jody, unsure why Mr. Barrett looked so disapproving. She had a horrid, sinking feeling that Mr. Barrett still thought she might bring Peter bad luck if they became too close.

"There's nothing to celebrate," said Mr. Barrett scowling. "I've got to talk to you. Come on inside. We've had bad news."

Peter put Jody down softly and stared at his father.

Mr. Barrett turned and walked into the house without saying another word. Suddenly, Jody and Peter heard a sharp cracking sound, almost like a gunshot.

"What the . . . !" yelled Peter, running into the house with Jody close by his heels.

Mrs. Markson stood by the dining room table holding a bottle of champagne. Groucho and Chico, the two cats, were playing with the cork. Mr. Barret was standing with his hands up in the air.

Mrs. Markson poured the champagne into a glass and handed it to Mr. Barrett. "Here's to you and Pure Energy!" she said, raising her own glass in a toast.

Mr. Barrett put down his glass. "I wish I could drink it, but I can't."

"Oh, I'm sorry," said Mrs. Markson quickly. "I didn't realize that the doctors had asked you not to drink. Jody and Jake and I just wanted to share with you your good fortune."

"Some fortune. Misfortune is a better name for it," sighed Mr. Barrett, sinking into a chair.

"Dad, will you tell us what's wrong?" cried Peter. "When I heard that champagne pop, for a second I thought you had pulled out a gun."

"Peter, I'm a fighter. I'm not going to take this lying down. I would never do a thing like that. But we've got a fight on our hands. The steward called me early this morning and they're calling an inquiry on Pure Energy's win. They say that this 'sudden reversal to form' is suspicious. My license is suspended and so is yours. We aren't even allowed in the backstretch until after the inquiry. This has never happened to me in twenty years in this business."

"Wait a minute," said Mrs. Markson. "They suspend your license *before* the inquiry? That isn't fair. It's like handing out the sentence before the trial."

"Racetrack inquiries aren't like a court of law," said Mr. Barrett. "The racetracks are afraid of scandal because there are so many ways to fix a race. In our business you're *guilty* until you prove you're innocent."

"But that's medieval," said Mrs. Markson.

"It's horse racing," said Mr. Barrett. "But I'm glad you feel that way. I'm going to need a lawyer. I was hoping that you would take my case."

Mrs. Markson nodded. Then she caught Jody's eye. Jody was signaling her mother to come into the kitchen so she could talk to her alone.

91

"Excuse me, Mr. Barrett," said Mrs. Markson, "I just want to check and make sure that Jake doesn't need any help in the kitchen. We all still have to eat. Jody, can you come with me?"

"Sure, Mom," said Jody.

When they got into the kitchen, Mrs. Markson turned to Jody. "Honey, I know how much you care about Peter and Mr. Barrett, and I'm going to do everything I can to help them. You look so upset, but you've got to cheer up. Being upset won't help them."

"No, Mom," said Jody, "it's just there's something you've got to know about. Peter told me his dad bet $500 on Pure Energy. He made nearly $50,000 on the race."

Mrs. Markson swallowed hard.

"$50,000!" screeched Jake in a high-pitched whisper. "And we didn't bet a penny."

"Shhh," said Mrs. Markson. "Well, no wonder the stewards suspected him of a fix."

"That doesn't mean he's guilty," said Jody loyally.

"No, but it doesn't mean he's innocent either," said Mrs. Markson sternly. "I wonder why he didn't tell me about the bet himself."

15

WASTED
BLUEBERRY
PANCAKES

It was one of the most unpleasant breakfasts Jody could remember. Mr. Barrett and Peter barely picked at Jake's special blueberry pancakes. Jake didn't even make a pun. The champagne sat on the table getting flat.

"I think we'd better talk," said Mrs. Markson finally. "I've never handled a racetrack case before. What is the procedure?"

"Well, the stewards will ask questions around the track. They'll probably write to England for some background on Pure Energy's racing form there. Basically, they think that I somehow instructed Peter to hold Pure Energy back on his earlier races so we could clean up in this race."

"And did you clean up?" Mrs. Markson asked directly.

Mr. Barrett blushed a deep red. "I don't want to talk about that," he said fiercely.

"But I'm your lawyer," said Mrs. Markson. "Anything you say to me is confidential. Jody, Jake and Peter, I'd like you to go outside for a while, if you don't mind. I need to talk to Mr. Barrett by myself."

"Come on," said Jody.

Jake looked at all the half-eaten food on the table. "What a waste," he said. "Do you all realize that those were great blueberry pancakes?"

"Come on," insisted Jody. "We'll have another celebration when Peter and Pure Energy win again; then the whole world will have to admit it's no fluke."

"That'll be the day," said Peter cynically.

"You wait," said Jody.

Outside, Peter kicked so furiously at a rock that it went flying into the air. Harpo chased it thinking it was a stick, and it barely missed his nose.

"I'm sorry, Harpo," said Peter, running over and making sure he was all right. "I didn't mean to take it out on you. I'm just so angry. *Finally*, it looked as if things were going great. Now, they're even worse than before."

"Hey, wait a minute," said Jody. "The stewards told your father in person, but they haven't told you. You can still go to the stables. You haven't been officially warned off."

"What good will that do?" asked Peter. "As soon as they see me, they'll warn me off."

"But that will give us a chance to look around," said Jody. "There's something very fishy about this whole thing. I want a chance to see Pure Energy for myself."

"Watch out," Jake warned Peter. "When she starts investigating *I* usually end up in trouble."

"But I get results," said Jody. "That's what counts. Come on, we've got to get to the stables. We'll just try to avoid the stewards. They will have no way of knowing whether your father got a chance to see you."

"First she gets you involved in a mystery," said Jake. "The next thing you know, Jody will have you walking on a ceiling to solve it."

"I never asked you to walk on a ceiling," protested Jody. "Now, let's go. Peter, you can't just sit back and let them take your license away."

"You're right," said Peter. "Let's go."

When they got to the track Peter waved at Buster as if nothing was the matter and drove right on through the gate, not leaving Buster the opportunity to stop him.

"Good going," said Jody. "Now, all we have to do is make sure we don't run into any of the track officials."

The backstretch looked strangely deserted on the Sunday after the big race. Jody, Jake and Peter walked across the track.

"I can't believe it was only yesterday I felt on

top of the world," said Peter savagely. "It seems so unfair."

As they walked toward the stable, Jody suddenly shouted, "Look! Who's riding Pure Energy?" She pointed to the far end of the track where Pure Energy was being ridden around the training track at an exceedingly fast gallop.

"What the . . . ?" exclaimed Peter. "Who's riding him? He shouldn't be having a workout today. Dad gave strict orders that he shouldn't be taken out of the stable today. He needs a rest after yesterday."

Peter ran across the track as fast as he could, with Jody and Jake right behind.

"Hey, you!" shouted Peter, unable to see the jockey's face half hidden under his western hat. "What are you doing on that horse?"

Peter arrived at the rail of the training track. The rider brought the horse to a walk. It was Betsy Hart, one of the best young jockeys at the track.

"What's the matter, Peter?" she asked.

Peter stared at her. She was riding an all-chestnut horse that looked exactly like Pure Energy.

"I'm sorry, Betsy," said Peter. "For a second, I thought you were riding Pure Energy."

Betsy laughed. "I wish I were. Congratulations on yesterday. You rode that horse perfectly."

Peter nodded, grateful that Betsy hadn't heard yet about his being warned off. If she hadn't heard, perhaps others didn't know about it either.

"Come on," said Peter to Jody and Jake. "It

was just a case of mistaken identity. Let's get to the stable."

"It's funny," said Jody, "from a distance I was sure it was Pure Energy."

"It fooled even me," said Peter.

When they got to the stables, Pure Energy was safe in his stall. He showed no interest in Jody when she went up to him and tried to pat his muzzle. "I guess horses have a short memory," said Jody. "I think he forgot me."

"He probably still has a swelled head from yesterday," said Jake. "He must think he's too good for you."

"Listen, you," Jody said playfully, patting Pure Energy on the neck. "I was the first person you bit in this country. You'd better remember me. I've got the scars to remember you."

Just then, Harpo slipped into the stall. Before Jody realized what was happening, Pure Energy lashed out with his front leg and sent Harpo flying into the wall of the stall.

Harpo lay there stunned, not moving.

16
MISTAKEN IDENTITY

Jody ran to Harpo and picked him up. He lay in her arms like a rag doll. It had happened in a split second. Jake and Peter stared at Harpo, horrified. He looked dead. He lay in Jody's arms limp and still.

Jody put her ear to Harpo's side. "He's alive!" she cried. She didn't even realize that tears were streaming down her face.

"Quick!" said Peter. "We've got to get him to Dr. Connelly. Because it's Sunday, none of the vets are at the track. I'll drive you."

Jake picked up an old horse blanket and helped Jody wrap Harpo in it to keep him warm. They drove to the vet's in virtual silence. Just as they were pulling into Dr. Connelly's driveway, Harpo began to whimper.

"He's coming to! He's coming to!" said Jody. She half jumped out of Peter's car in her rush to get Harpo to Dr. Connelly.

"Where is the doctor?" cried Jody as she ran into his office.

"Uh . . . he was just showing a visitor around," said Dr. Connelly's assistant. "What's the matter?"

"My dog just got kicked by a horse. He was knocked out, but he's coming to. I don't know if any bones are broken."

"Lay him on the table," said the assistant. "I'll call up and see if he's at the house."

"Please hurry," said Jody impatiently.

The assistant went to the phone. He put it down seconds later. "He's not up at the house. He must be around the grounds somewhere. Why don't you go look for him, and I'll start examining your dog." The assistant began gently probing Harpo's rib cage.

Jody stood over him as if rooted to the spot. "Come on, Jody," said Peter gently, "let's go find the doctor."

Outside the infirmary Jake twirled around, taking in the doctor's land. "I forgot the doc has such fancy digs."

"Yeah. Vets do very well around racetracks," said Peter. "I told you they make more money than trainers."

"This is no time to stand around chatting," insisted Jody. "We've got to find the doctor." Jody brought her hands to her lips and cupped them. "Doctor Connelly . . . Doctor Connelly!" she shouted at the top of her lungs.

Her voice bounced off the barn. "That should bring him," said Jake. But nobody answered Jody's call.

"Maybe he drove somewhere," said Jake.

"He could be in the barns," said Peter. "I'll go look." Peter started off toward the main barn.

"Come on, Jody," said Jake, "you and I can go to that small barn."

Jody and Jake ran down the hill toward the small barn. As they were turning around the corner, they careened into Dr. Connelly and Dr. Grant.

"What in the world . . . ?" cried Dr. Connelly.

"What are you doing here?" screeched Dr. Grant in a high-pitched voice.

For a second, Jody was taken aback. "It's Harpo," said Jody quickly. "He was kicked by Pure Energy and knocked out."

"Where?" said Dr. Connelly anxiously.

"He's up in your office," said Jake quickly.

"No, I mean where was he kicked," said Dr. Connelly, running up the hill.

"Oh, in his side," explained Jody. "He was knocked out for the whole drive up here, but just before we turned into your driveway, he seemed to come to."

Dr. Connelly turned to Jody. "I meant where was he when he got kicked."

"Oh," said Jody, not understanding why that was so important. "He was kicked at the racetrack. We were in Pure Energy's stall."

Dr. Connelly sighed a deep breath of relief. He glanced over Jody's head at Dr. Grant. She too seemed strangely relieved.

Inside Dr. Connelly's office, Harpo was still lying on his side. But when Jody ran to him, his tail began to thump weakly against the table, and his eyes opened.

"How is he?" Dr. Connelly asked his assistant.

"He's just coming around," said the assistant. "He certainly had the breath knocked out of him, but I can't tell if there are any internal injuries."

Dr. Connelly began probing Harpo's rib cage with gentle but experienced hands. Harpo winced once or twice. Jody held him steady. She looked up at Dr. Connelly with anxious eyes.

"I want to take some X rays," said Dr. Connelly. "Jody, he seems to trust you the most. You stay with him while I put the film in the machine. You won't have to move him off the table." Dr. Connelly went to the sink and washed his hands, which seemed to be stained with black oil.

"I was just working on some darned machinery in that old barn," said Dr. Connelly, as if he were trying to make conversation to take Jody's mind off Harpo. Jody knew that internal injuries in a dog could be terribly serious. Harpo could be bleeding to death inside, and there might be nothing that Dr. Connelly could do to save him.

Dr. Connelly took a series of X rays and handed them to his assistant. "Develop these right away," he said. "I want to find out if we have to operate." Dr. Connelly smiled at Jody. "Relax, dear. Dogs are much hardier than we think." Dr. Connelly patted Harpo on his head. Harpo's tail didn't even respond.

Jody bent down and pressed her face into Harpo's fur.

"Maybe he'll be okay," said Peter.

At the sound of Peter's voice, Harpo wagged his tail strongly. Harpo raised his head and licked Jody on the face. Jody laughed—the first laugh she had given since Harpo had been knocked out.

Jake grinned. "Hey, I think he's coming around."

Dr. Connelly came out of the darkroom. "Good news," he said. "The X rays show there are no broken bones."

"And he just licked Jody on the nose," said Jake.

Dr. Connelly smiled. "That's usually a sign that the patient is getting better. I think I should keep him for a day or two for observation—just to make sure that there's no internal bleeding. But I think it's going to turn out just fine."

"Thanks, Dr. Connelly," said Jody.

"Well, now if you'll excuse me," said Dr. Connelly, "I'm afraid I left Dr. Grant rather rudely. You can give me a call tomorrow to find out how Harpo is."

"Great," said Jody.

Dr. Connelly turned to Peter, as if noticing him for the first time. "Peter, I wanted to tell you how sorry I was about you and your father being warned off. I'm sure there's some logical explanation and that you and your father are innocent."

"Thank you, sir," said Peter.

"Well, I've known your father for many years and I've never known a more honest man. Even if Jared desperately needed money—and we all know how high hospital expenses are these days —he would never stoop to fix a race."

"I wish everybody felt like you do," said Peter. "I'll tell my father what you said. I'm sure it will cheer him up."

"I wonder what Doc Connelly would say if he knew Peter's father made close to $50,000 on that race," whispered Jake into Jody's ear.

"Shhh," warned Jody.

Dr. Connelly shepherded them outside. Down the hill, by the small barn, Dr. Grant was leading out a horse.

"Is that Dr. Grant's new racehorse?" Jody asked.

"Uh . . . no . . ." said Dr. Connelly. "That's just an old nag we keep around for pleasure riding."

The horse whinnied and stretched his neck

toward them. Something in his stance struck Jody as familiar.

"For a second, I thought it was Pure Energy," said Jody, half laughing. "I've been making that mistake all day today." When Jody looked up she realized that Dr. Connelly was looking at her with a deadly serious expression on his face.

17
NOT MUCH
TO CELEBRATE

Jody was silent as they drove back.

"Shall we go back to the stables?" asked Peter.

"Huh?" said Jody, as if she were coming out of a daydream.

"Are you with us?" asked Jake. "I get the feeling that you're in outer space."

"No. I was just thinking," said Jody. "I think we should go back to our house. Mom and Mr. Barrett will wonder what happened to us."

"Yeah," said Jake bitterly, "we were real successful at solving this mystery. We saw a horse that looked like Pure Energy. We got Harpo knocked out."

"It's like fighting a ghost," said Peter. "It's not

really a mystery. It was a lucky fluke, but now everybody is treating it like a mystery."

"You're wrong," said Jody. "I think it is a mystery. I've got an idea how it was done. First, I've got to ask you a question. When did Pure Energy start to act like a horse that could win?"

"What do you mean?" asked Peter.

"When I first started taking care of Pure Energy, you and your father laughed at the idea of his being a winner. You made fun of me when I thought he could win his first race."

"I never thought he could win," said Peter defensively.

"But your father must have. Why would he have bet $500 if he didn't think Pure Energy had a chance?"

"I don't know," said Peter stubbornly. He gave Jody a look, warning her not to push him further on this subject.

Jody sat back and watched Peter drive. "Peter," she said softly, "we can't help you or your dad if you don't trust us."

Peter's face softened. "I don't know why dad bet that $500," he said in a voice barely above a whisper.

"You don't suspect him of fixing the race, do you?" said Jake in a shocked voice.

"I wish I knew what to think," said Peter. "I know we desperately needed money, but Dad's a proud man. He wouldn't even talk to me about his debts."

"Peter," said Jody sharply, "you've been so busy worrying that your father is guilty that you aren't thinking straight. Come on, tell me the truth. When did Pure Energy start acting like a different horse?"

Peter practically drove off the road. "What are you getting at?" he demanded.

"When we saw the horse at the racetrack that looked like Pure Energy, I began to think," said Jody. "Horses do look alike. Suppose somebody switched horses on you?"

"You're crazy," said Peter. "That would be impossible. All racehorses have a tattoo on their lips, just to make sure that nobody ever tries to switch a fast horse for a slow horse."

"Besides," said Jake, "Peter was riding him. He'd be able to tell the difference. And I took care of the horse."

Jody got a stubborn look on her face, a look Jake knew only too well. "Peter, you said you believed Pure Energy had just improved. You would be so happy that Pure Energy was running better, you'd never think that it might be a different horse. If a fast horse suddenly became slow, you might grow suspicious. But if a slow horse becomes fast, it's natural to think that the horse just improved. And, Jake, no insult intended, but you don't really know horses very well. Whoever set up this switch was obviously an expert."

"Jody, you're snatching at straws," protested Peter. "Nobody could have switched Pure Energy."

"Wait a minute, Peter," said Jody earnestly. "Listen to me. I was probably the one who knew Pure Energy best and I was fired."

Peter pulled into the Marksons' driveway. He looked very thoughtful. "You know, I thought Pure Energy acted like a different animal when he came back from Dr. Connelly's. But you're right; I was so happy that he was running fast, I put the thought out of mind."

"And shortly afterward, someone convinced your father that I was accident prone. We've got to find the original Pure Energy, and I have an idea where he might be. Remember when I got knocked out at Dr. Connelly's? I was down by that old shed, near where we saw that horse today. I think that's where the horse could be. We saw Dr. Grant down there today. If I suspected anyone, I would suspect her. She would be in the position to do it. After all, Pure Energy is her horse."

"And exactly how do you expect to prove any of this?" demanded Jake.

"Well," said Jody, "the first thing I want to do is investigate that shed. We have to go back to Dr. Connelly's tomorrow to pick up Harpo. I'll just have to think of a way to get in there."

Jody was just getting out of the car when Mr. Barrett opened the front door of the Marksons' house. He had a set, grim expression about his mouth.

He ignored Jody and Jake, went around to the driver's seat and practically pushed Peter aside. "Where were you?" he muttered. Before Peter could answer, Mr. Barrett gunned the motor and they drove off.

"I'll call you," shouted Peter.

"That's not what I call a friendly leave-taking," said Jake.

"I know," said Jody. "Mr. Barrett looked angry. I hope Mom didn't tell him she couldn't take his case."

Inside, Mrs. Markson sat at the dining room table, looking thoughtful. "I'm afraid we didn't have much of a celebration," she said.

"What was Mr. Barrett so upset about?" asked Jody. "He took off out of here like he couldn't wait to get away."

"He's not going to be an easy client," said Mrs. Markson. "He's a very proud man. For some reason he refuses to discuss the bet he made."

"Well, it's not illegal for a trainer to bet on his own horse," said Jody.

"Yes, I know that's technically true, but I'm not going to be able to defend him in front of the stewards unless he tells me his reasoning behind the bet. Mr. Barrett doesn't seem to trust me, and if he doesn't trust his own lawyer, it's like tying my hands behind my back."

"Well, maybe he needs time. He's had a lot of hard blows lately," said Jake.

"Time is the one thing we don't have. If this were a court case, it would drag on for months. I'll say one thing for those racing stewards. They believe in swift justice. They've set a hearing for Wednesday."

"Did you talk to them?" asked Jody. "Do you think Mr. Barrett has a chance?"

"I talked to them all right. They acted offended that Mr. Barrett would even go to a lawyer. Unless I come up with something more than I've got, I think he's in trouble."

"What do you have?" asked Jake. "Did Mr. Barrett offer any proof that he's innocent?"

"I think he's too much in shock to realize what's happened," said Mrs. Markson. "My only hope is to get character witnesses to testify to his good reputation. But I have a feeling I'm going to need a lot more than that if he's to keep his license."

"Mom," said Jody, "do you think he's guilty?"

Mrs. Markson looked appalled. "That's a terrible thing to ask me about one of my clients."

"Come on, Mom," urged Jake, "it's a fair

question. You've had clients that turned out to be guilty."

"That's true," said Mrs. Markson, "but I put up a good fight for them and I'll put up a good fight for Mr. Barrett."

Jody looked at Jake. "I think Mom just answered my question," she said softly.

18
NO TIME
FOR A JOKE

Jake felt himself falling. He tried to grab the saddle, but he was rocking back and forth and he missed. "Jake! Jake!" Jody whispered urgently.

Jake opened his eyes. He felt the sheets around him. "Wake up!" whispered Jody.

Jake grunted. A wave of relief hit him as he realized he was in his own bed. "I dreamed I was falling off a horse," Jake said sleepily.

"Are you awake?" Jody demanded.

"Three cheers for the world's stupidest question," grunted Jake. "Of course I'm awake. You just woke me. What time is it?"

"Four thirty."

"Four thirty!" exclaimed Jake.

"Shhh," said Jody. "I don't want you to wake up Mom."

"I'm glad you're considerate of someone. Why

did you wake me up at four thirty in the morning? I think that qualifies for cruel and unusual punishment."

"Come on," said Jody, "you're the one who's supposed to be the early morning person."

"Four thirty qualifies as middle of the night," said Jake self-righteously.

"I couldn't sleep. I kept worrying about Peter and his father."

"Couldn't you have worried just a couple of hours more by yourself?" said Jake.

"No. I've thought of a plan. We've got to try to find Pure Energy. As soon as whoever did it realizes we suspect a switch, they'll kill the original Pure Energy. He's the only piece of evidence."

"What makes you think he's not dead already?" asked Jake.

"Even a second-rate racehorse is a pretty valuable piece of property," said Jody. "Somebody, most likely Dr. Grant, discovered two racehorses that looked alike. We'll call the winning Pure Energy, Horse X. Horse X must have papers and a good bloodline, or he would never have been able to win the Gold Cup. Our culprit has now switched Horse X for Pure Energy. They can still sell Pure Energy under Horse X's papers."

"Jody!" interrupted Jake, "you can't just wake a person up out of a sound sleep and start talking about Horse X."

"All right," said Jody, "then just get up. Put on

dark clothes and sneakers. We don't want any-body to see us if we can help it."

When Jake got downstairs Jody was waiting for him, dressed in a light, black cotton turtleneck and jeans.

"Exactly how are we going to get there?" asked Jake.

"I called a taxi. I decided we'd better leave Peter out of this for a while. I don't want him to get into any more trouble."

"Personally, I wouldn't mind staying out of trouble myself," said Jake. "What exactly are we going to do?"

"First, we're going to have to go to the race-track and take a look at the winning Pure Ener-gy's tattoo. Then we're going to Dr. Connelly's."

"I'd say that's a full pre-dawn schedule," said Jake. "If I fall asleep later and really fall off a horse, I'll blame you."

"With any luck, we'll have this mystery solved by breakfast," said Jody confidently.

"Modesty has never been one of your virtues," said Jake.

"Let's go," whispered Jody. "I hear the taxi."

Buster Harris was sound asleep in his chair by the gate when the taxi drove up. He woke up with a start.

"Hi, Buster. It's just me, Jody Markson. I left something at the Barrett's stable that we need this morning . . . uh . . . my wallet. We're just going over there for a moment."

Buster looked confused. "It's awful early," he said.

"I know," said Jody with a smile. "But you know how panicky you get when you think you've lost your wallet. I just have to find it."

"Sure, sure," muttered Buster, as if he didn't want to talk anymore.

"I don't think Buster is an early morning person," said Jake.

Jody told the taxi driver to wait for them as they hurried over to the Barrett's stable.

Pure Energy was sleeping standing up when Jody tiptoed up to his stall.

"Now, all you've got to do is get him to curl his lip," whispered Jake.

Pure Energy shook himself at the sound of Jake's voice and opened his eyes.

"Easy, boy, easy," whispered Jody gently. She stepped inside the stall. Pure Energy stood docilely. "Be careful," warned Jake. "Remember what happened to Harpo."

Jody lifted Pure Energy's upper lip. "A-133151," she read.

"Sounds like a Social Security number," said Jake.

"Did you write it down?" asked Jody.

"Yup," said Jake.

"Okay, let's get back to the taxi."

When they were driving out to Dr. Connelly's, Jake glanced at the meter. "$4.85!" cried Jake.

"This is going to cost us a mint before we're done. Who's paying for it?"

"I got money from my salary working for Mr. Barrett," said Jody. "And besides, if we're successful, Mom can charge it as expenses."

"And if we're not, we're out the money," said Jake. When they got a block from Dr. Connelly's, Jody told the taxi driver to stop.

"We'll walk from here," she said.

"Do you want me to wait for you again?" asked the cab driver.

Jody started to say yes, but Jake put a hand up.

"No," he said quickly. "We don't know how long it'll take us, and it's stupid to pay all that money. There's a telephone by the gas station."

"You sure you kids don't want me to wait?" asked the driver. "It's still pretty dark out."

"We'll be all right," said Jody.

As the cab drove away Jake said, "I wonder what he thought we were doing, traveling around by cab everywhere."

"Maybe he thinks we're jockeys," said Jody.

"I just hope he doesn't think we're horse thieves. By the way, what are we going to say if somebody catches us at Dr. Connelly's? Or are you planning just to make something up at the moment?"

"We'll just tell them we were worried about Harpo," said Jody. "I'll say I couldn't sleep thinking that Harpo must be missing us. Lots of owners are crazy about their pets."

"How does that explain what we are doing in the shed?" asked Jake.

"Uh . . . well, it will do as a starter," said Jody. "Besides, I'm not planning on getting caught."

"Good," said Jake, "I find that very reassuring."

"We'd better stop talking now," said Jody as they came to the edge of Dr. Connelly's property.

"Somehow, I feel like I should be putting on a mask," whispered Jake.

"Shhh," said Jody as she began to crawl through the bushes. "This is no time for jokes."

"I wasn't joking," said Jake.

19

"WHOA, BOY! WHOA"

In silence they scurried past the darkened main house. There was no moon, and once they were out of the reflection of the street light, Jake could barely see Jody in front of him. They kept to the grass so that their sneakers would make no sound on the gravel driveway.

Once past the main house, Jody and Jake ran in a half crouch down the hill to the shed. Jake could feel his heart pounding in his chest. He was sure it was pounding loud enough to broadcast that they were there.

"Here," commanded Jody. "Take the flashlight. You have to shine it on the lock for me so that I can see what I'm doing!"

Jody held out the flashlight. It was wrapped in

black tape so that its shiny aluminum surface wouldn't reflect any light.

"You really came prepared, didn't you?" whispered Jake.

"Shhh," said Jody as she examined the large combination lock holding the shed door closed.

The sound of their whispering voices woke up the horse inside. He whinnied softly, almost as if he recognized their voices.

"You'd better think of something quick," said Jake, "or that horse is going to wake someone up."

"We're going to have to go in through the window," said Jody, pointing to a small window that looked as if it dropped directly into the horse's stall.

"Oh, terrific!" said Jake. "Suppose he's keeping some killer horse in there and you just happen to drop in on him."

"Jake! Stop talking and give me a lift."

Jake cupped his hands to take Jody's foot and hoisted her so that she could grab the window's ledge with her hands. Jake handed her the flashlight. She pulled herself up. Jody's guess was right. The window did lead directly into the horse's stall. She eased it open and slipped inside.

She could feel the warm, almost hot, breath of the horse right next to her. "It's okay . . . it's okay," Jody whispered frantically, with images of Jake's 'killer horse' flying through her brain. The horse seemed to take her presence in his stall with remarkable calmness. *Even a nonkiller horse,* thought Jody, *would be justified being nervous about my dropping in on him from above like some equine Santa Claus.*

Jody shone her flashlight over the horse's flank. He looked the same chestnut color as Pure Energy.

"Jake!" she whispered as loud as she dared.

"Are you all right?" he whispered back.

"Yes, but I need you to hold the flashlight while I look at his tattoo. Can you get up to the window by yourself?"

Jake let out a deep sigh. "We're going to get caught. I know it," he muttered. But he pushed a bale of hay under the window and started to climb through.

"Where is the horse?" demanded Jake.

"He's keeping nice and quiet. Don't worry about him. I'm sure it's Pure Energy and he's recognized my voice."

Jake landed in the soft straw.

"Hurry!" said Jody. "I've got to check his number quickly. I just know the number is going to be same."

Once again Jody grabbed the horse's muzzle. This time the horse started to back away nervously. "Whoa, boy! Whoa!" whispered Jody. The horse calmed down at the sound of her voice. Jody curled his lip up and Jake flashed the light.

His teeth were badly stained various shades of brown. The numbers on his lip stood out clearly.

$$8188151.$$

"It's a different number," hissed Jake.

Jody stared at the numbers in disbelief. She had been so sure this horse was the original Pure Energy.

20
HORSE X

"You've been wrong before," said Jake philosophically. They were sitting by the gas station, having escaped out the window and back up the hill.

Jody had her head in her hands. "But I was so sure I was right."

"You've been that before too," said Jake dryly.

Jody took her head out of her hands and gave him a dirty look. "That's more natural," said Jake.

"I guess I was just barking up the wrong tree," said Jody.

"Or betting on the wrong horse," said Jake. "Speaking of barking, we still have to pick up Harpo today. Are we going to call a taxi and then come back for Harpo?"

"What time is it?" asked Jody.

"Ahh . . . I'm glad you asked me that," said

Jake. "It happens to be almost dawn. Five forty-five. Nothing like a rich full night to make you appreciate a full day's work."

"I think we should go back to the racetrack," said Jody. "After all, we haven't been warned off. Maybe we can still pick up some useful information. We can take the bus."

"Don't you think we'd better call Mom?" said Jake. "She's liable to have woken up in the middle of the night and thought we were kidnapped."

"Whoops. You're right," said Jody. "I never thought of that. She's such a good sleeper in the morning, I just figured she wouldn't even realize we were gone. I'll call her."

The phone rang ten times before Mrs. Markson picked it up. She grunted into the phone.

"Mom?" asked Jody tentatively. "You sound as if you're in the bottom of a metal bathtub."

"Where are you?" asked Mrs. Markson.

"Uh . . . we're out, Mom . . . both Jake and I are going to the racetrack. We didn't want you to worry," explained Jody.

Mrs. Markson was not quite awake enough to pick up the gaps in Jody's explanation. "Fine," she muttered. "I have to go to the track today myself. I'll see you there."

"Great," said Jody. "Bye." As Jody hung up she could hear her mother begin to wake up and say, "What are you two doing out before dawn?", but by that time Jody had softly put down the receiver.

Jody and Jake took the bus back to the race-track. Buster Harris rubbed his eyes when he saw them. "Am I dreaming?" he asked. "Didn't you already come in?"

"Isn't it a beautiful day?" said Jody, not wanting Buster to make too much of their comings and goings.

"You're getting awfully good at changing the subject," whispered Jake.

Buster nodded at them as they passed through the gates.

"Have a nice day, Buster," Jody shouted cheerily.

"You sound like a telephone operator," muttered Jake.

"Will you stop picking on me?" complained Jody.

"I'm not picking on you," said Jake. "Well," he admitted, "maybe I am, just a little. I think my nerves can't quite take all this pre-dawn adventure."

"I guess the real Pure Energy is stashed someplace else," said Jody. "And I haven't the slightest idea of where to look."

Jake looked extremely worried. "You're not planning a series of 4 A.M. morning-raids, are you?" he asked.

"I'm not sure exactly what we should do," said Jody.

When they got to the barn Peter was leading

Pure Energy out for his morning rubdown. Peter squinted into the sun when he saw them.

"Hi," he said. "Thanks for showing up. I'm sorry my father left in such a huff yesterday. He's real upset."

"How come you're here?" asked Jake. "I thought if you were warned off you couldn't come to the track."

"Apparently even the racing stewards relented. They called late last night and told my father that in view of his past record he could continue at the track until the inquiry was held. We can't, of course, enter any races, and I'm not allowed to race, but they will graciously allow us to muck out our stalls and take care of our horses. Wasn't that nice of them?" Peter added sarcastically.

"How did your father take it?"

"Badly," said Peter. "I thought he was going to have another heart attack on the phone. I talked him into taking a sleeping pill last night and staying in this morning."

Pure Energy, or Horse X as Jody preferred to call him, seemed to grow restless as Peter was talking.

"Will you hold him?" asked Peter, handing the reins to Jody.

Peter brought out a bucket of hot water that smelled of mint from the soap. Pure Energy shook his head and rolled back his lips. "He seems nervous this morning," said Peter. "He was wide-awake when I came in, pacing around his

128

stall." He picked up the aluminum sweat scraper to scrape off the excess soap.

"Uh . . . well, maybe he's still excited from winning the Gold Cup," Jody suggested.

"That might have been the biggest mistake of your life," Peter said to the horse as he moved to the far side. "I wish we had a tape recording of Dad trying to talk Dr. Grant out of entering him. Then maybe the stewards would believe him that he didn't expect Pure Energy to win."

Peter handed the scraper to Jody so that she could do her side. Jody liked the easy sharing she felt with Peter. She loved the smell of the peppermint from the soap and the rich earthy horse smell. She realized with a start that this would have been the best summer in her life if it hadn't been for the horse standing in front of her.

"Peter, has anybody ever switched a fast horse for a poor horse in a fix?" asked Jody.

"I told you before, Jody, that switching horses would be impossible," said Peter. "You can forget it. I know your reputation as an amateur detective, but you won't get anywhere with that theory. It can't be done."

"Why?" asked Jody. "Horses do look alike."

"The tattoos," said Peter. "You're right. Switches apparently used to happen fairly often in the old days. But since the Racing Commission has insisted on the tattooing of all thoroughbreds at birth, it would be impossible to pull a switch."

"Are race horses tattooed in England?" Jody asked thoughtfully.

"You know, I don't know," admitted Peter. "But even if they aren't, a horse would be tattooed as soon as he entered the country.

"I guess you're right," said Jody, sounding discouraged.

"Hey," said Peter with a smile. "You're the one who's supposed to be cheering me up, remember. I'm the one who's been warned off. Come on. I've got to walk Pure Energy, and we've got other chores to do."

21
A LONG SHOT

A couple of hours later, Liz Gerber showed up.

"Good morning!" shouted Liz Gerber. She stuck her head in the barn. "Is anybody here?"

"Hi!" said Jake, coming out of an empty stall. "Peter and Jody are taking a couple of horses for some exercise. I've been left to mind the shop."

"You're Jake Markson, aren't you?" asked Liz Gerber. "Your mom asked me to meet her here."

"Can I get you a cup of coffee?" asked Jake, glad of any excuse to stop mucking out the stall.

"Sure," answered Ms. Gerber.

Jake brewed the coffee in the tack room and handed it to Liz Gerber.

"You're the kid who's good at figuring out odds, aren't you?" she asked.

Jake blushed. "How did you find out about that?" he asked.

"Gossip is my business," said Liz Gerber. "You can't be a good handicapper unless you spend a lot of time sorting out all the different things you hear."

"I just like to make pretend bets," said Jake.

"They're the best kind," said Ms. Gerber. "If Jared had stuck to pretend bets he wouldn't be in the trouble he is in now."

"Uh . . . does Mr. Barrett have a reputation as a heavy gambler," Jake asked.

"No . . . talk about your 'sudden reversal of form,' Jared Barrett hardly ever made a bet. I think that's one of the reasons the stewards are looking into this race so closely. Your mother asked me to meet her here this morning. I understand she is Jared's lawyer. She has some questions she wanted to ask me."

Just then Mrs. Markson stepped into the tack room. Peter and Jody were with her, having met her coming in from their exercise gallop.

"Thanks for meeting me," said Mrs. Markson. "I know so little about racing, I needed to talk to an expert. I realized something very curious last night. When I went up to make a bet I didn't have to give my name to the ticket taker."

"That's right," said Liz Gerber. "It's all done with computers these days. You pay your money up front. If you lose, the track just keeps your money. If you win, you cash in your ticket."

"But what about taxes?" asked Mrs. Markson.

"Those are taken out before you get your

money," said Liz Gerber. "There's no cheating the income tax people."

"So, betting can be very private. Nobody has to know who bet on what horse. Yet everyone seemed to know about Jared's bet."

"Ahh . . . that's the advantage of our grapevine system here," explained Liz Gerber. "Either Jared told somebody or someone saw him in line picking up his winnings."

"But that's exactly the point," exclaimed Mrs. Markson. "If Jared had really fixed the race he easily could have hidden the fact that he placed a bet on Pure Energy. The very fact that he didn't keep it a secret points to his innocence."

"But it doesn't prove he's innocent," said Liz Gerber.

"Right now, it's the only straw I've got," said Mrs. Markson. "Do the racing stewards know who else bet on Pure Energy?"

"No," said Liz Gerber. "As I said, all betting is anonymous today."

"But you could find out whether there were other big bets, couldn't you?" suggested Jody, speaking up for the first time. She had been sitting quietly in a corner playing with a pencil and paper.

"Why, yes, I guess so," said Liz Gerber. "The computer keeps track of the amount bet on each horse because, of course, we change the odds depending on how much is being bet."

"I see," said Mrs. Markson. "So if a lot of people decided to take a gamble on Pure Energy for the Gold Cup, his odds would have gone down."

"Right," said Liz Gerber. "And we know that the odds went down only a little from 85-to-1 to 80-to-1."

"But Mr. Barrett's bet of $500 wouldn't have been enough to bring it down five points," said Jody. "Somebody else must have bet on Pure Energy."

"Well, some people always like to bet on long shots," said Liz Gerber. "They have fantasies of the *big win.*"

"But you could find out whether it was a bunch of small bets or one big bet on Pure Energy that brought the odds down, couldn't you?" insisted Jody.

"Yes, we could do that." Liz Gerber looked at Mrs. Markson. "If you think it's important, I could check it out."

Mrs. Markson turned to Jody. "I think I know what Jody is getting at. Yes, I think it would be very important to know if anybody else made a killing on Pure Energy."

22

A CLEVER IDEA

"Your hunch was right," said Mrs. Markson the next day. "Liz Gerber just called me. Two people made $1,000 bets on Pure Energy. That's $162,-000 paid out. The bets were made very near post time and didn't change the odds because almost nobody else bet on Pure Energy, including me, I might add."

"Come on, Mom," said Jake, "stop beating a dead horse."

"Yuk!" exlaimed Jody. "No dead horse jokes. What are you going to do, Mom?"

"I wish I knew. The inquiry is tomorrow. I'll mention these bets, of course, and I'll try to build up the case that Persons X and Y would have had even more of a reason to fix the race than Jared. But I'm building up only a circumstantial case. I don't have any hard evidence. Mr. Barrett and Peter are coming over today to go over their case, but frankly, I think there is a very good chance they will lose their licenses."

"Mom, can we sit in on your conference with Mr. Barrett and Peter. I have a theory that I want to tell you about."

"I'll have to ask Mr. Barret and Peter if it's all right with them," said Mrs. Markson. "After all, *they* are the clients. But you do have a legitimate interest, and I have to admit your question to Liz Gerber was a good one."

"Better watch it, Mom, Jody may take your business away and go into business for herself," warned Jake.

"First she'll have to go to law school, and if either of you kids want to come into practice with me, nothing would make me happier."

Just then the doorbell rang. The Marksons all looked at each other. It was something of a family tradition to argue about who would get the door.

"It's probably your clients," said Jody to her mom.

Mrs. Markson turned to Jake. "Peter was your friend before any of us knew him."

"Yeah, but he's turning into Jody's boyfriend," said Jake.

"That's not true," protested Jody in a high voice.

"That was hitting below the belt," said Mrs. Markson. "For that *you* go get the door, Jake."

Jody gave her brother a grin as he got up to get the door.

Mr. Barrett and Peter walked in together. Mrs. Markson stood up and shook Mr. Barrett's hand firmly. "Jody has asked if she and Jake could sit in on our meeting. She and Jake feel very involved, and I have to admit, Jody has given us one good lead." Mrs. Markson told the Barretts about the discovery that two other people had made a fortune on Pure Energy.

"Have you found out who they were?" Peter asked anxiously.

"No," admitted Mrs. Markson. "I just got the information from Liz Gerber this morning."

"Nobody else is going to be as stupid as I am," said Mr. Barrett angrily. "They'll keep it quiet."

"Well, that's the one thing we have going for us," said Mrs. Markson.

Peter laughed uncomfortably.

"Oh no," said Mrs. Markson, "I didn't mean it the way it sounded. It's just that if your father had really fixed the race, he would have kept quiet about his earnings."

"At the time I was so excited that the horse won," explained Mr. Barrett, "I was willing to tell the world."

"Can you remember exactly who you did tell?" asked Mrs. Markson. "Word got around awfully fast. It might be important to know who told the stewards."

"Well, I remember I was standing next to Dr. Connelly, and I was so happy when Peter came across the finish line, we were hugging and carrying on like kids. I'm pretty sure I told him. And everyone knows Dr. Connelly can't keep a secret. I probably told some other people too."

"Good," said Mrs. Markson. "The more the better. I'm going to hammer that point home in front of the stewards. Now, you have to tell me why you decided to place that large bet on Pure Energy. If you want Jody and Jake to leave the room they will be glad to, but I'm your lawyer and anything you say to me is confidential."

Mr. Barrett just looked at the floor. "It's nothing that secretive," he muttered. "I just feel like such a darned fool. All my life I've preached against betting at the race track. I know it's the heart of our business, but I've just seen too many of my friends lose their shirts, lose their businesses, ruin their marriages. Why, some people even call me 'the preacher' around the racetrack because I take such a high moral stand—get up on my high horse, if you know what I mean."

"Yet, you decided to bet $500 on Pure Energy at tremendous odds?" said Mrs. Markson puzzled. "Why I even let Jody talk me out of a $2 bet."

"But I've never seen a horse change so much before," said Mr. Barrett excitedly. "After I had my heart attack, I know many people thought I had lost my touch. Yet, here was a horse who came to me an obvious loser, and in just a few short weeks, I had turned him into a winner. In my whole life, I've never seen anything like it. When we got that horse, I wouldn't have given you a plug nickel for his chances. But when he came back from Dr. Connelly's he started to look like a real racehorse."

"Are you sure it was the same horse?" Jody asked.

"Don't be silly," snapped Mr. Barrett. "Of course, it was the same horse.

Throughout the conversation, Jody had been scribbling on a piece of paper. Jake tried to get a look at what she had written. Jody stabbed at her notebook with her pencil, but she didn't say anything else.

Mrs. Markson glanced at Jody curiously. "Jared, I'd like to talk to you alone. I've got a lot of work to do to prepare for tomorrow's inquiry. Peter, why don't you join us in a little while." Mrs. Markson and Mr. Barrett left the room.

Jake looked at his sister. "You don't give up easily do you," he said. "I thought we had disproved the switched horse theory." Jake told Peter how they had investigated the horse in the shed.

Jody continued to draw very deliberately in her notebook. "I've been playing with those numbers all day," she said excitedly. "I didn't want to tell Mom and Mr. Barrett until I could be sure. But if you put the numbers underneath each other, you'll see something very strange."

Pure Energy: A133151

Horse X: J188151

"The tattoos are done in block letters, and using block letters you can easily change an "A" to a "B" and a "3" into an "8".

Jake peered over Jody's shoulder at her notebook. Peter looked discouraged. "Jody, if somebody changed the tattoos the way you described, you'll never be able to prove it. You might as well forget it."

"I can't stand the idea that somebody is going to get away with this scheme and you and your father are going to have to take all the blame."

"I know," said Peter softly. "But there's nothing we can do."

"Oh, yes there is," exclaimed Jody.

"Watch it," said Jake. "When Jody gets that tone in her voice, we're all in trouble."

"Well, we can't just sit by and do nothing," said Jody. "And you're right. I have a plan."

23

A MIRROR IMAGE

"I wish your plans didn't always mean getting up in the middle of the night," muttered Jake. He looked at his watch. The digits read 2:29.

"I've got to admit, I could have used a good night's sleep myself," yawned Jody.

They were standing by the curb outside their house. A few seconds later, Peter drove up with a horse trailer attached to the station wagon.

Jody and Jake hopped in quickly.

"Did you have any trouble?" asked Jody, glancing back into the horse van. She could hear the sound of a horse stamping his feet impatiently.

"No. This part of the operation went smoothly," said Peter. "I decided to sleep at the stables. I often do that anyhow. Then I just loaded Pure Energy and drove out. Buster was half asleep when I left the gate, and he's used to my coming and going."

"Didn't he question the fact that you had a horse van?" asked Jake.

"Nope," said Peter. "I told him that I had to go pick up a horse for the track. And luckily, Pure Energy didn't make any noise at that exact moment."

"Luck is what we're going to need," said Jake. "I can't believe you let Jody talk you into this."

"Well, you're here too," said Peter. "Besides, I agree with Jody. It's our only chance."

Peter parked the horse van a block away from Dr. Connelly's house. "Okay," said Jody, "we'd better get to work on Pure Energy. Let's bring him out of the van so we can use the lights on the lamppost."

"What exactly are we going to say to any neighbors who happen to see a strange horse in the middle of the night?" asked Jake.

"It's not against the law to go for a ride at three in the morning," said Jody.

"Right," said Peter. "Just tell them you couldn't sleep."

"Well, that's the truth all right," muttered Jake.

Peter coaxed the horse in the van out into the street. He held the horse's head while Jody took a pen and printed in the changes on the horse's tattoo. It now read:

B188151.

"Where did you get a pen that would work?" asked Peter.

"I went to the stationery store and told the owner I needed a pen that could write underwater. He gave me something called the "space" pen. It can write on the moon and underwater and over grease. Maybe I should also write them that it can write on a horse too."

"Let's get moving," said Peter nervously. Jody and Jake walked beside the horse as Peter led it down the street. The sound of the horse's hooves on the pavement rang out loudly.

"We've got to get him on the grass," urged Jody. "All right now, I've found a path. No more talking."

Slowly and carefully, Jody led Peter and Pure Energy through the bushes to the side of the shed. "Okay, Jake," Jody whispered. "Hold the flashlight while I get out my screwdriver."

Working as fast as she could, Jody unbolted the hinges from the old barn door, opening it without disturbing the lock. Peter kept the horse happy and quiet by allowing him to pull straws out of a bale of hay.

Jody inched the door open. She took the reins from Peter, and then quickly led the horse into the shed. Peter followed her. Jake stayed as a lookout. For a second, Jody felt as if she had stepped into a mirror, like Alice in Wonderland. Facing her was a horse that looked exactly like the horse she was leading.

"We'd better not get mixed up at this moment, or we're in big trouble," whispered Peter.

"I know," whispered Jody. "It's strange, isn't it?" The two horses eyed each other warily.

"We'd better move fast," whispered Jake urgently, "before there's trouble between these two horses."

Peter moved quickly to the other horse and snapped a lead line to its halter. As he attempted to lead it past Jody, the horse she was holding flung its head in the air and gave a loud, challenging neigh.

Peter rushed his horse out of the shed before a fight could start. Jody unsnapped her lead line and quickly ran out of the shed. Both horses were excited now. The horse outside the shed pranced nervously, flinging its head around wildly. The horse inside the shed pounded the floor with its hooves.

"Quick!" Jody commanded. "Help me move the bale of hay."

Jake put all his weight behind the bale and rolled it out of the way. Jody moved the door back in place and deftly screwed the hinges back on. She almost had the last screw in place when she turned and saw a light go on in Dr. Connelly's house.

"Get the horse out of here," Jody commanded. "Jake, you go with Peter."

"What about you?" insisted Peter. "We can't leave you here."

"I've got a much better chance if you're gone," said Jody. "I'm almost through. If they catch us with the horse, we *are* in trouble."

"I don't want to leave you here," Peter said defiantly. "I'll finish screwing in the door. You go with Jake."

"Get out!" hissed Jody. "It's much worse if they catch you. You're in trouble already."

Jake saw the sense of Jody's argument. "Peter, she's right," urged Jake, grabbing Peter's arm. Reluctantly, Peter led his horse through the bushes. "We'll meet you by the gas station," whispered Jake.

Jody had just gotten the last hinge screwed in when she heard a noise coming through the bushes. Quickly she put the screwdriver in her pouch and ran up the hill. She had nearly gotten to the street when suddenly a giant light flashed in her eyes, momentarily blinding her.

"Who's there?" demanded a voice.

Jody put her hand up to shield her eyes. She looked around wildly, hoping against hope that Peter and Jake were out of sight with the horse.

24
CAUGHT IN THE ACT

Jody knew she couldn't run. The voice in the dark shouted again. "Who is there?" The light came closer.

"It's Jody Markson," said Jody in a shaky voice.

Jody thought she heard a curse. "What in the world are you doing here in the middle of the night?" demanded Dr. Connelly. He sounded furious.

Jody looked up at the sky as if hoping for divine intervention. Streaks of pink were showing on the horizon. Jody knew it must be near dawn.

"I can explain," she stammered. "I had a horrible dream about Harpo. I heard him crying for me in my sleep. It woke me up and I just knew I had to come to be near him. I know it sounds stupid, but I couldn't bear to lie in my bed and think about Harpo being all alone. Then, when I got here I felt so foolish. I didn't want to wake you up. So I was just standing in the driveway trying to think of what to do until you woke up."

Dr. Connelly looked at her as if he didn't believe her. "You'd better come inside with me," he said threateningly.

Jody knew she had better follow. She wanted to give Peter and Jake a chance to get as far away as possible. "All right," she said, swallowing hard.

"I'm so sorry I woke you up," she babbled. "Do you think I can see Harpo now? Is he all right? It was such a realistic dream."

"Your dog is fine," said Dr. Connelly flatly. He motioned Jody into his office. Apparently, Harpo heard the sound of her voice for he suddenly started barking furiously from his cage.

Jody went to Harpo's cage. He seemed delighted to see her, wagging his tail so hard he kept thumping it against the side of his cage.

"I'm so relieved that he's all right," chirped Jody, hoping that she sounded silly enough. "I can't tell you what a scary nightmare it was. There was a monster in it who was going to eat me . . . and I just knew Harpo's spirit was calling to me."

Dr. Connelly didn't seem to be listening to Jody, which of course was exactly what she was hoping for. He paced around his office. "I think I'd better call my mother and tell her where I am," said Jody shyly.

Dr. Connelly gave her a suspicious look. "I wonder what she thinks of your wandering around before dawn."

"She understands about me and Harpo," Jody explained. Jody dialed her home number. She knew she had to do something fast before Peter and Jake became so worried that they came to rescue her. The phone rang several times before Mrs. Markson picked it up.

"Mom," said Jody, "it's me. Uh . . . this is hard to explain, but I'm at Dr. Connelly's."

"Jody!" exclaimed Mrs. Markson. "It's not even 6 A.M."

"Uh . . . yes, I'll explain all about it when you get here," said Jody quickly. "Please hurry. And oh, I forgot to tell you that you need gas. Luckily, there's a gas station right near Dr. Connelly's. If you hurry there now, they'll be open."

"Jody," warned Mrs. Markson, "what are you babbling about? Are you all right?"

"No," said Jody softly into the phone, holding the receiver close so that Dr. Connelly could not hear her mother's response.

"All right," said Mrs. Markson, suddenly very wide awake. "I'll be right there." Jody put the receiver back on the hook.

"My mom will be here right away," Jody said. "I'm really sorry to have disturbed your sleep."

Dr. Connelly narrowed his eyes to look at her. Jody knew he thought she was lying, but he didn't know exactly what she was lying about.

The next ten minutes were probably the most awkward Jody could ever remember. She sat in a chair with Harpo by her side. Dr. Connelly sat opposite her. He wasn't holding a gun, but the feeling was as if he were. They didn't exchange more than ten words. Clearly, Dr. Connelly suspected that she was up to something, but he had no proof.

Jody felt a wave of relief flood over her when she heard her mother's car turn into the driveway. She was followed by Peter in the station wagon, trailing the horse van. Jody felt her heart beating very fast. She knew the next few moments would be crucial.

Mrs. Markson got out of the car. "What's going on?" she demanded. "I ran into Peter and Jake on the road."

"Mom," said Jody calmly, "can you call the racing stewards? I think I can prove that Dr. Connelly has hidden a double of Pure Energy in his shed."

"Why you little deceiving, lying, brat!" shouted Dr. Connelly.

Mrs. Markson looked at Dr. Connelly in shock. Then she looked at her daughter. "Jody," she said softly, "do you know what you're doing?"

"I'll sue her for libel," threatened Dr. Connelly. He turned his fury on Mrs. Markson. "If you listen to your daughter, I'll sue you also."

"Dr. Connelly, Jody wouldn't make an accusation unless she could back it up. Besides, I was going to have you called before the racing stewards in order to take a deposition from you anyhow. I understood that you were the one who spread the story that Mr. Barrett had won a lot of money on Pure Energy."

"It wasn't a story," protested Dr. Connelly. "It was the truth."

"We're not denying that," said Mrs. Markson, "but it is pertinent to determine exactly whom you told. I think I will call the racing stewards. From what I've seen of racing hours they'll all probably be up anyhow."

By now Dr. Connelly was so furious he could hardly speak. "Perhaps," said Mrs. Markson, "it would be better if Jody and I waited in the car." Mrs. Markson half grabbed Jody's arm to drag her into the car.

"Jody, do you know what you are doing?" asked Mrs. Markson anxiously.

"Yes, Mom," said Jody. "There's a look-alike of Pure Energy in Dr. Connelly's shed. The horses were switched, and Mr. Barrett didn't know a thing about it. I had to switch the horse's back without letting Dr. Connelly know about it."

"You shouldn't have trespassed," said Mrs. Markson.

"I know," said Jody, "but otherwise he would have gotten away with it."

"You know two wrongs don't make a right, Jody," said Mrs. Markson.

"But technically, I wasn't trespassing. I'm the

owner of a dog Dr. Connelly is treating, and I came to check up on him."

Mrs. Markson laughed. "Well, I don't think Dr. Connelly has early morning visiting hours, but I guess you're right. Let's go find out what's happening. I just hope your switch has worked."

25
A RACE
TO THE FINISH

"It is simply a retired racehorse that I keep for my friend," insisted Dr. Connelly, as he led a procession down to the shed. The racing stewards had arrived, bringing along Dr. Grant and Mr. Barrett. Mrs. Markson and Jody followed a few steps behind. Jake and Peter trailed them at a respectful distance. Jody had her fingers crossed the entire time. She knew that the trap she was trying to pull off was so complicated that a dozen things could go wrong, and she was more worried than she ever remembered being in her life. If she failed, there would be no way of covering it up. It would be horribly embarrassing for her, and devastating for Peter and Mr. Barrett.

Dr. Connelly swung open the door to the shed. Jody held her breath, scared that she hadn't put the hinges back on right. She had visions of the door coming off in Dr. Connelly's hands, making it obvious to everyone that the shed had been tampered with.

But the hinges held. Dr. Connelly led out the horse in the barn. It was clear to everyone that the horse looked exactly like Pure Energy. But, Dr. Connelly turned to Jody scornfully. "I suppose as an *amateur* detective you became overexcited when you saw a horse that looked like Pure Energy, but it simply proves you have little or no experience around horses." Dr. Connelly turned to the racing stewards. "As you gentlemen know, to the untrained eye, horses frequently look alike. Perhaps young Miss Markson didn't realize that for precisely that reason we tattoo all racehorses. If you check the tattoo on my horse you'll see it is a different number from the horse that won the Gold Cup."

Jody held her breath as the racing steward lifted the horse's lip so that he could see the number. The steward wrote down 8188151. Then he looked at his slip of paper. "Dr. Connelly is right," he announced. "This horse's number is not the same as Pure Energy's."

Jody breathed a sigh of relief. The trickiest part of her plot was over. She turned to the racing steward. "I understand that it is the veterinarians who tattoo the numbers. Dr. Connelly has probably done thousands of tattoos. He would have discovered which numbers could be easily changed. For example, Ⴙl33l5l could be changed to 8l88l5l. I have a wager to make with Dr. Connelly. He says that the horse he is holding is just a retired racehorse who isn't very fast. If he will allow his horse to race the Pure Energy that is in Peter's trailer, we will see which horse will win."

A big smile spread across Dr. Connelly's face. He knew that Jody was wrong. She would never prove anything by such a race. Dr. Connelly was sure that the horse he was holding was the slow Pure Energy, the one who couldn't win a race if his life depended on it.

"I will take you up on that wager, young lady," said Dr. Connelly. "If you will agree to drop all charges against me if you are proven wrong. I cannot have you going around the racetrack slurring my reputation."

"Dr. Connelly is being more than fair," said the racing steward.

"I agree," said Jody. "If the horse in the Barrett's trailer can beat your horse, I will admit that I was wrong and that you had nothing to do with the fix."

"There's a small abandoned half-mile track in my back field," said Dr. Connelly. "We can have the race there. If that's all right with you," he added sarcastically to Jody.

"Anywhere will do," said Jody.

"Just make sure we remember which horse is supposed to be which," whispered Jake as they walked down to the ring. Dr. Connelly led the horse from his shed. Peter led the horse from his van. No one spoke. Jody had the feeling that everybody expected her to make a fool of herself.

"All right," said Dr. Connelly, obviously having decided that *he* was going to take charge. "It's silly to make too much of this. Who exactly is going to do the riding? Peter is obviously the most experienced rider. I think he should ride my horse. Jody is a pretty good rider, and she should have no trouble just staying on top of the horse that won the Gold Cup. She can ride the winner. The rest of us will watch the riders closely to make sure that no cheating is involved. It's a small ring, so we'll be able to see everything they do."

"That's all right with me," said Jody.

Mrs. Markson looked worried. "Jody," she said, "are you sure you will be all right. You aren't really a trained jockey."

"I'll be fine," said Jody, sounding nervous.

"It'll be okay, Mrs. Markson," said Peter. "A race is much less dangerous when there are only two horses. It's when there's a field of a dozen or two that it's really dangerous, and I have an extra helmet in the car. We'll both wear helmets." Peter handed Jody a helmet. "Good luck," he whispered. "Just don't fall off."

"I won't," said Jody. "May the best horse win," she said in a loud voice. Jody mounted her horse. As she adjusted her stirrups, she caught Dr. Connelly glaring at her. Jody stared down at him. Suddenly, she felt flushed with confidence that her plot was going to work. Towering above the others just because she was on a horse and in a saddle, Jody felt as if she understood why generals had statutes made of themselves on top of a horse. It was a marvelously powerful feeling.

Peter and Jody walked their horses around the ring once in order to loosen them up and to get a feel for the track. "Be careful," warned Peter, "the track is in lousy condition." Jody looked down at the deep divots and clods of crabgrass.

"Come on, you two," shouted Dr. Connelly. "Let's get this stupid charade over with." Dr. Connelly drew a line in the dirt with a stick. "This will be the start and finish line," he said. "We don't have a gun, so line up in back of the line and I'll wave a handkerchief for the start."

Jody gripped the reins nervously. "It's okay," Pure Energy. You're going to do your best." She knew she was on the original Pure Energy, the horse who had bitten her, the horse who had arrived from England in such bad shape. Dr. Connelly raised his handkerchief in the air, but before he could lower it Harpo suddenly darted out from Jake's side and onto the track.

"Get that stupid dog out of there!" commanded Dr. Connelly

Peter's horse completely ignored Harpo, but Jody's horse shook his head up and down and whinnied happily. "Go away, Harpo," whispered Jody, worried that Harpo might give away the whole scheme if Dr. Connelly remembered which horse was supposed to like Harpo.

Jake ran out to the track and dragged Harpo back to the other spectators. "Hold on to him," warned Jody.

Dr. Connelly raised his handkerchief again. "ON YOUR MARK. GET SET. GO!" he shouted, dropping his handkerchief.

Jody kicked her horse hard in the flank and loosened the reins an inch. Her horse responded by leaping forward. Peter's horse broke into an immediate gallop, but Jody was able to keep him close. All of a sudden all the complexities of the switched-horse con game fell away. It was simply a race between two horses that happened to look exactly alike. For Jody and Peter the outside world disappeared. They were locked in a very real race, and Jody wanted only to win.

She bent down low so that her mouth was practically in Pure Energy's ear and she urged him to go faster. The ground sped by so fast that Jody had trouble keeping her breath, and each time she asked Pure Energy for more speed she felt him gather himself together and push harder.

Yet Peter was slowly inching away. His horse had barely worked up a sweat. As they made the turn, Peter opened up a clear lead, first three lengths, then six, then eight.

Jody's horse put his heart into trying to catch up, but he didn't have the strength. "It's all right! It's all right," Jody whispered as she tried to hold him together.

26
JODY'S
DARK HORSE

"You tricked me!" shouted Dr. Connelly in fury. "You little brat. Somehow you switched horses on me *again*. The horse in my shed should never have won."

Peter had pulled his horse up to a walk after crossing the finish line. His horse was barely breathing hard. Jody came up. Her horse was wheezing and blowing air in and out. He had obviously tried his hardest but had not been able to come near Peter's horse.

Mrs. Markson picked up the crucial word. "Again?" she asked mildly.

Dr. Connely was so furious he didn't realize what he was saying. "Yes. Somehow your daughter set a trap. She switched the horses back again."

"Shut up," said Dr. Grant, realizing too late what Dr. Connelly was saying.

Dr. Connelly whirled around. "Were you in on it? Perhaps you thought we were going to be caught, and you arranged this little trick."

"I don't know what he's talking about," protested Dr. Grant. "I had nothing to do with any con game. All I did was buy a racehorse."

"Oh no you don't," said Dr. Connelly. "You're in it as much as I am. You can't sneak out."

Jody dismounted and handed the reins to Jake. "I did fool you," she admitted. "But I had no choice. You and Dr. Grant had been too clever. I knew what you had done, but I didn't know how to expose you, so I had to pull a double switch in the hopes that you'd spill the beans."

"Why you double-crossing little sneak!" exclaimed Dr. Connelly. "You little twerp, you ruined a foolproof plan."

"Well, your foolproof plan meant ruining the reputations of two people I care about," said Jody defiantly. "You chose Mr. Barrett because you knew that he was recovering from a heart attack. Somehow you found *two* horses in England that looked alike, but had vastly different abilities. You realized you had the makings of the classic racehorse switch. One horse could run and get a reputation as a dud so that the odds on him would be awful. Then you could switch horses and clean up. As the veterinarian involved, you could easily do the tattoos in block letters that could be changed. All you needed was someone to put the blame on."

"I shouldn't have just knocked you out when you came sneaking around that day," said Dr. Connelly. "I should have knocked you out permanently."

"That's enough threats," said the racing steward. "I thought this girl and her mother were crazy when they called me this morning, but it turned out they were right." The racing steward turned to Mr. Barrett, who looked pale. "Jared, we owe you an apology."

"I still can't believe it," muttered Mr. Barrett. "Doc Connelly was my friend."

"He had developed very expensive tastes," said Mrs. Markson. "He saw a way to make a lot of money. Dr. Grant was willing to put up the money to buy both horses. She is as guilty as he is, and they couldn't resist the temptation to clean up."

"The racing officials are going to have quite a time trying to sort out the records on this mess," said Mr. Barrett. "Switches like this have happened before. I don't envy them their job."

Mr. Barrett walked over to Jody's horse and felt his legs. "Jody, that horse put out for you. He really tried. He kept up with Peter's horse longer than I would have ever expected."

"Now what's going to happen?" asked Jody.

"Well, while the racing officials and the law figure out the legal snafus we've got two horses to take care of. No matter what, a horse has got to be taken care of—even if he's a bum. And your horse has proven he's not a bum. He was outclassed today. We've got to find a race that will bring him confidence. I'll try to match him with other horses where he can beat them. And if your mom is willing, I think you're the person who should ride him. Horses are athletes. Don't ever forget that. They have to compete! And if you can get an athlete to beat somebody, he'll want to beat other people. This horse could turn out to be a winner yet."

"But what's his name?" asked Jody. "We can't keep calling them both Pure Energy."

"I've got a name for him," said Peter. "I think he should be called Jody's Dark Horse. After all, if Jody hadn't masterminded the double switch, we would probably both be out of racing permanently."

"I think that's a great name," said Mr. Barrett. "And I know I'll never forget what I owe Jody and all the Marksons."

"Does that mean I have my job back?" asked Jody teasingly.

"Yup," said Jake. "It means that you get to wake up before dawn every morning this summer again. Now aren't you happy?"

Jody groaned.

ABOUT THE AUTHOR

ELIZABETH LEVY grew up in Buffalo, New York, and was graduated with honors from Pembroke College. She is a versatile writer of both fiction and nonfiction, including *Lizzie Lies a Lot, Lawyer for the People* and *The Case of the Frightened Rock Star: A Jody and Jake Mystery* #1. "Jody and Jake" is her first mystery series for older readers. She is also well known for her popular "Something Queer Mysteries." *Publishers Weekly* says: "Levy excels at the invention of baffling comedy mysteries."

Coming from Archway in the future is *The Case of the Fired-up Gang: A Jody and Jake Mystery* #3.

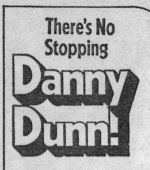

There's No
Stopping

Danny Dunn!

Danny Dunn, science fiction hero, with his friends Irene and Joe, can't stay away from mystery and adventure. They have shrunk to the size of insects, traveled back in time, sunk to the ocean floor, and rocketed through outer space!

**The DANNY DUNN books
by Jay Williams and Raymond Abrashkin:**

_____	29983	$1.75	Danny Dunn and the Smallifying Machine No. 1
_____	29984	$1.75	Danny Dunn, Invisible Boy No. 2
_____	29985	$1.75	Danny Dunn, Scientific Detective No. 3
_____	41495	$1.95	Danny Dunn and the Universal Glue No. 4
_____	29974	$1.75	Danny Dunn and the Homework Machine No. 5
_____	29972	$1.75	Danny Dunn and the Swamp Monster No. 6
_____	29975	$1.75	Danny Dunn and the Anti-Gravity Paint No. 7
_____	29971	$1.75	Danny Dunn, Time Traveler No. 8
_____	29967	$1.75	Danny Dunn on the Ocean Floor No. 9
_____	29966	$1.75	Danny Dunn and the Weather Machine No. 10
_____	29968	$1.75	Danny Dunn and the Fossil Cave No. 11
_____	29970	$1.95	Danny Dunn and the Voice From Space No. 12
_____	29977	$1.95	Danny Dunn and the Automatic House No. 13
_____	29969	$1.95	Danny Dunn and the Heat Ray No. 14
_____	29976	$1.95	Danny Dunn on a Desert Island No. 15

Meet McGurk!

Got a mystery to solve? Just ask McGurk. He heads the McGurk Detective Organization, and he and his supersleuths—Wanda, Willie, Joey, and Brains Bellingham—can unravel just about anything! They've solved the puzzle of the ruthless bird killer, tracked down a missing newsboy, traced an <u>invisible</u> dog, and cracked the case of a mysterious robbery.

Can you solve these tricky cases?
Follow the clues and
match wits with master-mind McGurk!
The McGURK MYSTERIES, by E. W. Hildick, illustrated by Iris Schweitzer.

YOUNG LOVE,
FIRST LOVE
Stories of Romance